Cheryl,
Thank you!
Loved meeting you!
Jenna!

JENNA ST. JAMES BOOKS

Ryli Sinclair Mystery Series Order

Picture Perfect Murder
Girls' Night Out Murder
Old-Fashioned Murder
Bed, Breakfast, and Murder
Veiled in Murder
Bachelorettes and Bodies
Rings, Veils, and Murder
Last Stop Murder

Sullivan Sisters Mystery Series Order

Murder on the Vine
Burning Hot Murder
Prepear to Die

DEDICATION

To the Falcon. Yes, I know it's an object, but it's the central object of Ryli's life. It is the very thing that drew Ryli and Aunt Shirley together. And it's one of the real-life cars my sister, Juliana, owns. When the Santa Rosa, California fires hit all around my sister's house, she texted to tell me they were told to evacuate and that she would have to leave the 1965 Ford Falcon behind because she could only take one of her vintage cars—she had many to choose from. I was heartbroken. The fires danced all around her house for over a week (within two blocks), but luckily, she and the Falcon were spared.

To Donn Harrison. Thanks for always answering my EMT/firemen/police questions…and when you don't know the answer, you hook me up with someone who does. You are the best!

CHAPTER 1

"I still can't get over Garrett's pre-wedding gift to you." Aunt Shirley twisted the earbuds in place then adjusted her safety goggles. "The Glock .40 is definitely a good choice for you. Lightweight and easy to grab."

I laughed. "That's exactly what Garrett said when he gave it to me."

While I was thrilled with the gift, I knew it symbolized more than just my soon-to-be police chief hubby, Garrett Kimble, giving his soon-to-be wife, Ryli Sinclair, a gun. It meant he was coming around to my desire to get my PI license. Aunt Shirley had taken her test and passed one week ago, and now I was itching to join in the ranks. I was still waiting on my background check to clear, but once that was done, all I needed to do was take the two-hour test. Aunt Shirley had been drilling me nonstop every day on what I could expect on the test.

"And the fact he's letting me shoot with you says a lot," Aunt Shirley continued as she tilted forward on her hips. "It shows how much he's willing to embrace our new career path."

I rolled my eyes. "I don't have a new career path yet. Just because I've decided to go ahead and get my PI license doesn't mean I'm choosing a new career path."

"Honey, you already submitted your application and have been fingerprinted. All you need to do is take the test to be licensed. It's a new career path."

4

I was saved from arguing as Aunt Shirley sighted the gun and fired off a couple rounds at the makeshift target.

Impressive!

Aunt Shirley laid the gun down on the wooden platform in front of her, yanked off her goggles, and pulled the earbuds from her ears. "Whoowee, just like old times. The first two were a little right of the target, but the third hit the bullseye!"

"Nice shot." I picked up my travel mug of hot tea and took a sip.

And it really was. My first night shooting with Garrett wasn't nearly as impressive as Aunt Shirley's shots. Of course, Aunt Shirley had years on me there.

My seventy-five-year-old, great-Aunt Shirley had run away to Los Angeles when she was in her early twenties to become a private investigator in a time when that wasn't the norm for women. She'd bucked tradition and had never gotten married nor had children. Well, until recently…the married part, not the children part.

"It sure would be fun to shoot some of your pumpkins," Aunt Shirley said lightly.

"No way!"

Aunt Shirley pouted. "It's not like anyone's gonna see them out here in the middle of nowhere. I bet you won't even get one Trick-or-Treater come out here."

I shrugged. "No skin off my back…more candy for me to eat. I've been trying so hard the last two weeks to follow a strict diet so I can still fit into my wedding dress on Saturday!"

Aunt Shirley cackled. "We *might* have overdone it a little in Las Vegas for your bachelorette party. But it sure was fun."

Fun wasn't the F-word I used when I came back from the Vegas trip and tried to zip up my wedding dress. I got it zipped…I just couldn't breathe. So for the last two weeks now I've been on a strict caloric intake, and I've even went jogging a couple times

5

with Garrett in the early mornings. Which wouldn't be so bad if the cold, October air didn't burn my lungs and give me coughing fits.

"You probably should have started that regime more than fourteen days before your wedding day, you ninny." Aunt Shirley sauntered over to sit next to me in one of the chairs on the back deck of Garrett's house.

And my house.

I needed to get used to thinking of this place and both of ours seeing as how we were to be married in four days.

"Your chunking up aside," Aunt Shirley said, "you holding up okay otherwise?"

I let out a quick laugh. "I'm not chunking up! Geez, I put on a few pounds is all!"

Aunt Shirley ran her gaze over me then shrugged. "Lover boy seems to like you no matter how you look, so I wouldn't stress too much over your—"

"Stop! Can you please just stop talking about my weight."

"Not much else to talk about then, is there?" Aunt Shirley flicked the top row of her false teeth out and then sucked them back in.

"Gross. And yes, there's plenty to talk about. Like how's married life treating you?"

Aunt Shirley had recently married Old Man Jenkins on a drunken binge in Las Vegas the night of my bachelorette party. No one was as shocked as Aunt Shirley when she woke up the next morning sporting a wedding band on her ring finger.

Aunt Shirley scowled at me. "I don't wanna talk about that low-down rascal. I still haven't forgiven him for tricking me into marrying him."

I hid a smile behind my mug of hot tea. In truth, Old Man Jenkins didn't have to trick Aunt Shirley too much. I think she wanted to marry him, she was just too darn stubborn to admit the truth to herself.

6

"But you've moved in to his apartment at the Manor and you're all settled in, right?"

Aunt Shirley shrugged then reached up to pat her hair. "You haven't said anything about my new hair. Don't you like it? I did it special just for your wedding. Matches your wedding colors."

I ran my eyes up to her hair. Aunt Shirley has been known for her outrageous, colorful hairstyles for a while now. Usually it's pink and purple. Today it was striped with strands of burgundy, deep purple, and orange.

"It's lovely," I said, keeping a straight face as best I could. "Now, stop trying to change the subject. Are you all moved in to Old Man Jenkins'ss apartment?"

"Yes, you know I am!" Aunt Shirley huffed and looked out across the pond in our backyard. "He's annoying, you know. He makes messes he doesn't clean, he thinks he's *always* right, and he snores!"

"You could be talking about you right now. You know that, right?"

"Hush your mouth and respect your elder."

I laughed. "You forget you moved in with me for a little while a few months ago. I know how hard it can be to live with you."

Aunt Shirley crossed her arms over her sagging chest. "If all I'm gonna get is grief, I might as well go home."

I didn't rise to her bait. "Is that what you want? To go home to your man? Maybe fix him a little supper and rub his feet."

Aunt Shirley shot me the death glare. "Watch your mouth or I'll turn you over my knee."

I bit my lip to keep from laughing. Nothing got Aunt Shirley riled up more than having to admit her feelings for Old Man Jenkins.

"Let's put the gun away," I said, "and I'll drive you back to the Manor."

Aunt Shirley sighed. "I miss the Falcon. Now that I've gotten my PI license again, I miss not being able to jump in the Falcon and tail bad guys."

The Falcon Aunt Shirley was referring to was the 1965 turquoise Ford Falcon she drove for over thirty years. It had purple ghost flames you could barely see, and under the hood was a stock 302 with an Edelbrock fuel injection. The barely-there dashboard was done in the same turquoise color, and the bucket seats in the front and bench seat in the back were pristine white with turquoise stitching. It was her pride and joy for decades, and now the Falcon is *my* pride and joy.

I smiled but didn't say anything. I may not be able to identify with her feelings, but I understood what she was saying. "Maybe soon you and I will be tailing bad guys together."

I saw the hopeful gleam in her eye and it made me proud. I've struggled with my decision to get my PI license. After all, in a few days I'm getting married to an ex-military hottie and the current police chief who had no idea I had other plans in mind when he asked me to marry him. I know Garrett loves me unconditionally, but he's also ten years older than me. He wants to start a family and lead a quiet, unassuming life. Yet when I look at Aunt Shirley and the life she's led, I feel such a tug on my insides. I've pretty much lived my whole life in Granville, Missouri, population ten thousand. Attending college was the only time I'd ever left Grandville. And while I love Garrett with all my heart, sometimes I yearn for more. And God bless him, even though he didn't sign up for a wife who had suddenly decided to change career paths, he's going with it.

Or so he says.

"You haven't mentioned anything about me not smoking my e-cig," Aunt Shirley said. "You probably haven't even noticed. Some PI you'll make."

I rolled my eyes. "I actually *did* notice you haven't had it for a while. I get why you didn't take it to Vegas—what with you being under constant scrutiny of Mom. But why haven't you smoked it since you've been back?"

Aunt Shirley shrugged and avoided my gaze. "Just because. I don't have to have a reason."

I smiled wickedly. "I bet it has to do with your new hubby. What's the matter, Aunt Shirley, Old Man Jenkins put his foot down on puffing inside the apartment?"

"You hush your mouth! I don't give two poots what that man thinks."

I bit my lip to keep from taunting Aunt Shirley even more. I knew when enough was enough.

"I need to stop by the pharmacy on our way home tonight," Aunt Shirley said.

"Why? Are you not feeling well?"

Aunt Shirley grinned wickedly at me, her false teeth practically glowing in the approaching twilight. "Gotta renew the old man's Viagra prescription. I mean, I'm angry at him…just not *that* angry."

I shuddered and stabbed at my eyes, trying to erase the image that popped up.

***

I jerked awake, my heart pounding wildly in my chest. I flung my arm out to grab on to Garrett and have him soothe my fears…only to find Garrett's side of the bed was cold.

I glanced over at his side of the bed.

Empty.

I donned my robe and silently walked down the curved, wooden staircase that Garrett had painstakingly made by hand, through the living room, and into the kitchen. A few years ago, when Garrett moved to Granville to take the chief of police job, he'd bought the small country house on a few acres and completely gutted it. Now it was a beautiful structure with cathedral ceilings, a stone fireplace, modern kitchen, and one-acre pond.

"Morning," I whispered.

Like always on these early mornings, I was tempted to kiss his cheek and make him feel better. But I never did.

He looked up from his coffee to smile at me. "Morning, Sin. You're up early."

"As are you. Everything okay?" I already knew the answer, but I thought I should ask anyway.

He gave me a small smile and shrugged. "Just a lot on my mind."

His usual answer when I asked.

I'd only recently taken to staying out at the country house semi-permanently. Before that, I stayed in town at my one-bedroom cottage my brother Matt owned. I'd honestly been oblivious to Garrett's sleep patterns—or lack thereof. I now knew he had difficulty sleeping most nights, and even though he never talked about it, I knew it stemmed from the life he'd led before coming to Granville…almost eight years on the police force in Kansas City and twelve years active duty in the Army. He'd already been enlisted when the world changed in September of 2001.

"Can I do something for you?" I asked tentatively, hesitant to touch him but still standing by his shoulder.

"C'mere." He wrapped his arms around my waist and pulled me down onto his lap. He didn't say anything more, just buried his head in my shoulder. We stayed like that for a few minutes, neither one saying a word.

"I could stay here like this forever," I whispered.

I felt his chuckle and release of breath against my neck. "Me, too. Although we wouldn't get much done."

"That's okay. I don't mind."

Garrett leaned me back and brushed my hair off my face and shoulder. "Ryli, you are so good for me. I don't even know the right way to tell you how much I love you."

Tears filled my eyes at his words. "And I love you, Garrett."

I jostled as he shifted my weight on his legs. "I never want anything to happen to you. I would give my life to keep you safe."

My heart dropped at his words. "Stop. Don't say things like that. Is it because I want to get my PI license that you're so upset this morning?"

"No, babe. I mean, I've wrestled with your decision to do this *crazy* thing with your *crazy* aunt," he grinned impishly at me, "but the truth is, it's one of the things I love about you. You're fearless and smart. And, besides, it wouldn't matter if you bagged groceries at the local supermarket, I'd still worry about you every day. I love you and want to always keep you safe."

"Promise me you'll remember those words in five years when you've had enough of me and you're looking for ways to bury my body."

Garrett chuckled. "I promise."

He upturned me and my feet landed on the kitchen floor. "Let's make some breakfast and get this day started."

"Anxious for the next few days to get here, are you?" I teased.

He didn't reply, just gave me a soft tap on my bottom.

Meow!

"Good morning, Miss Molly." I bent to pick up my black and white long-haired cat, nuzzling my face against her neck. "Got your food right here."

I scooped out a cup of her favorite food and placed it in her bowl. She leaped out of my arms and dug in.

Garrett and I spent the next few minutes working side-by-side in the kitchen. I got the food out of the refrigerator while Garrett started cooking. I strode to the coffee pot and poured a mug half full. Garrett's coffee was strong enough to put hair on my chest. I knew to only fill the cup half full and add enough cream and sugar to make it be real coffee.

"Did Aunt Shirley come over last night for target practice?" Garrett asked.

I took a sip of the coffee.

Perfect.

"She did," I said. "She's excited about helping you teach me to shoot."

Garrett grunted but didn't say anything more. "How are things at the new Andrews-Jenkins household?"

I grinned and took another huge swallow of my coffee. "Well, she complained nonstop last night about his snoring, his lack of housekeeping skills, and how she's still angry at his deceiving her…and then she had me stop by the pharmacy to pick up his prescription of Viagra."

Garrett flinched. "Oh, man. Please never do that to me again."

I giggled. "Just wanted you to have a little taste of what my life's been like lately."

Garrett filled our plates with bacon and eggs and kissed me as he carried them to the table. "Don't do me any favors."

The rest of the morning passed quickly as we ate our breakfast, washed dishes, then raced upstairs to get ready for the day. With it being seven days before Halloween, Hank had me doing a lot of themed pieces for the paper.

I was sitting on the bed watching Garrett get dressed for the day—something I never tired of doing—when his cell phone rang.

"Seven-thirty in the morning on a Wednesday," I joked. "Must be something good."

Garrett looked at the display and frowned. "It's Aunt Shirley."

I had just enough time to wonder why she was calling Garrett rather than me when he answered. "Morning, Aunt Shirley. Ryli's here and I have you on speaker phone. What's up?"

There was a slight pause. "Well, Ace, I need you to get down here to the Manor as quick as you can. There's been a murder."

My heart lurched at her words.

"Who?" Garrett demanded.

"Me."

CHAPTER 2

"What's the meaning of this, Aunt Shirley?" I demanded as I barged through her front door apartment at Oak Grove Manor.

Aunt Shirley had moved into the assisted-living facility about two years ago, but had recently taken up in Old Man Jenkins'ss apartment now that they were married. And his place was a lot more inviting than her old apartment had ever been. When my aunt first moved into the Manor, she refused to believe she'd be there long, so she never decorated. Two years later when she moved out, it was still as sparse as the day she moved in. Moving her things over to Old Man Jenkins's apartment had taken all of five minutes.

Aunt Shirley held up her hand. "Settle down there, Sunshine. No need to yell, I ain't hard of hearing."

Old Man Jenkins was standing in the small kitchen, his face telling me all I needed to know. Whatever it was…it was bad.

"What's going on?" I demanded again.

"It's nothing too serious." Aunt Shirley fanned a piece of paper in her hand.

"I beg to differ my dear bride." Old Man Jenkins's voice was as hard as gravel, and my heart leaped at his tone.

"Let's all sit down," Garrett said diplomatically. "See if we can't sort this out."

Aunt Shirley huffed then plopped down in a chair at the table. The three of us followed suit, my eyes never leaving the paper she was holding in her hand.

"Let's start with why you called me," Garrett said, "and informed me you'd been murdered."

I heard Old Man Jenkins's quick intake of breath, but Aunt Shirley waved him off.

"It might have been a bit dramatic, but that's basically what I got this morning. A death threat."

Garrett held out his hand. "Can I see it?"

Aunt Shirley hesitated for only a moment before she shoved the note at Garrett. I leaned over to take a peek.

Written in red block letters were the words: "I hear congratulations are in order. I hope this marriage isn't a grave mistake. D."

I furrowed my brow. "I see this as more of a vindictive letter. I honestly don't get sinister murderer out of that."

Aunt Shirley didn't meet my eyes. "You might when I tell you who it's from."

"Who?" Garrett demanded.

"Yeah, who?" I said. "It's not signed. Well, except for the D. And that could be anyone."

Aunt Shirley sighed. "It's a long story. I'll try and make it brief. About twenty-five years ago in ninety-two, I helped put away a mass murderer who was terrorizing women in Los Angeles. His name was Nicholas Wayne Danner. He was thirty years old, handsome, had a way with the ladies. The cops had dubbed him the Charismatic Killer. And even though he was only charged with two murders and one attempted murder, the Los Angeles Police Department believes he was responsible for at least four other murdered women…they could just never make a connection."

"That's horrible, Aunt Shirley," I said. "I had no idea you were involved in something that serious."

Aunt Shirley shrugged. "It was the main reason I went into retirement. Nearly thirty years on the job and I thought I'd seen it all. I decided after the trial to pull up stakes and come on back to Missouri."

"How does that story bring us to your death threat?" Garrett asked.

Aunt Shirley looked at Old Man Jenkins before answering. "I was the one that brought Nicholas Danner down."

My mouth dropped open. "How?"

"I'd been tailing him for two days. The police had narrowed their suspects down to three men, but I knew Danner was the guy. I followed him into a honkey-tonk bar and hid out while he drank and looked for his next victim. I noticed he was paying special attention to one of the waitresses, but she was so busy she barely gave him a glance. After he left, I decided to slip her my card and told her my suspicions about Danner, and if he came back she needed to call me immediately. I don't think she really believed me, but she slid my card in her uniform. I was on consult with the police department because they needed every available hand they could find. Two nights later I got a call from the Lieutenant in charge and he wanted me to tail another suspect. Even though I put up a fight, they pretty much demanded I ditch Danner and tail their other suspect. Three hours into my stakeout, I get a frantic call from the waitress at the bar. She said Danner was sitting in her section right now. She was terrified and wanted to know what she should do."

Aunt Shirley paused. I looked down at her hands and saw they were shaking. "Waylon, would you mind getting me a cup of coffee with a generous helping of that Irish cream?"

Old Man Jenkins cleared his throat and gave Aunt Shirley a small nod. "Sure thing."

"I told the waitress to sit tight. I'd be there shortly. I didn't call it in, because I knew the uniforms would tell me to stay on the guy I was tailing. So I just left my post and headed over to the bar." She reached out and took the cup of coffee from Old Man Jenkins. "By the time I got to the bar, she was nowhere in sight. The bartender told me she'd complained of a headache and clocked out."

"Why would she do that?" I asked. "Didn't she know he'd follow her?"

Aunt Shirley shrugged. "She just panicked, I guess. It took a lot of muscle, hysterics on my part, and a few death threats before the bartender finally give me her home address. I told him to call the police, and I lit out of there like the Falcon's butt was on fire."

I smiled at that image.

"When I pulled up to her apartment, the police hadn't arrived yet. I decided to go in. I couldn't wait around for the police…I'd seen the body of the last girl."

Aunt Shirley paused and took a long drink from her coffee mug. I could tell by her vacant eyes she was playing the scene all over again in her head.

"I had my gun on me, so I crept up the stairs and listened in at the door. When I didn't hear anything, I tried the knob. I almost wet myself in fear when it turned. Danner had been in such a hurry he'd forgotten to lock it. I pushed the door open and listened in. I could hear music from the stereo, which was his MO. He never gagged his victims because he liked to hear them scream, but the music helped drown out the screams enough so the neighbors wouldn't hear."

"That's just sick," I whispered.

Aunt Shirley nodded. "It is. I heard voices coming from down the hall. I figured they were in her bedroom. I honestly was going to wait a few more minutes until the police arrived, but then I heard her scream." Aunt Shirley closed her eyes for a moment. "I'll never forget that scream as long as I live. It wasn't so much a scream from terror as it was from outright pain. I ran down the hall, kicked in the bedroom door, and leveled my gun at that sorry piece of trash."

My hands blew up to my mouth. "What happened next?"

Aunt Shirley let out a hollow laugh. "I still see it in slow motion. I saw him straddling her, cutting her up pretty good, blood was everywhere. I just lost it. I screamed at him to get off her. He turned and looked at me with pure hatred. Like how dare I interrupt his play time. He came off that bed so fast, I hardly had time to blink. And he came straight for me. I screamed again for him to stop, but he kept coming, knife raised…so I shot him."

Aunt Shirley shook herself, as though waking from the memory. "Bullet went clean through his shoulder. He dropped the knife and a few seconds later the police came shoving their way through."

Garrett smirked. "How much trouble did you get into?"

Aunt Shirley grinned. "Quite a bit. But seeing as how I caught him in the act of flaying his next victim, the police were willing to look the other way."

I sighed impatiently. "How does all this get us to the death threat you received this morning?"

Aunt Shirley looked at Old Man Jenkins. I could read the guilt in her eyes. "The night of his arrest, and clear up through the trial, every chance Danner got to speak, it was to threaten my life. He basically said I'd be his masterpiece, but first I'd suffer loss like I'd never experienced before. I basically shrugged it off, just chalked it up to a crazed lunatic spouting garbage."

"But?" Garrett prompted.

Aunt Shirley sighed and turned to me. "Ryli, I know last week was the one-year anniversary of the first time you and I worked together to take down Sharon and her reign of terror on Granville. But what I never told you was there was a reason I was so eager to help you when you came to my apartment last year."

"And that was?" I asked.

Aunt Shirley looked again at Old Man Jenkins. "Stop frowning at me like that! I never said anything because it was no one's business but my own!"

"Aunt Shirley," I said, suddenly wishing I had a cup of coffee with lots of Irish cream, "what was the reason?"

"Every year during this time for the past twenty-five years I get a phone call from the Los Angeles Police Department letting me know my letter had arrived."

Garrett's eyes lit up with understanding. "And what exactly is in the letter?"

"A generic, yet cryptic note from Danner telling me how much I'm missed and he can't wait to see me again."

18

I gasped. "Wait, what? Isn't he in prison for life?"

Aunt Shirley let out a harsh laugh. "No, child. Things hardly ever work out that way. He was sentenced to twenty-five to life."

"Okay," I said as rationally as I could…because I could see where this was heading. "But he's still in jail, right? I mean, if he was released, you'd have said something, right?"

Aunt Shirley chewed on her lower lip. "Now don't go getting all excited."

"Not get excited!" I all but screamed at her. "Omigod! Where is he now?"

"He was released a couple months ago for good behavior. Plus, it seems he has terminal cancer and has been given less than six months to live."

"Good behavior?" I exclaimed. "He *murdered* women!"

Garrett ignored my outburst. "So if ever there was a time to strike, it's now."

Aunt Shirley nodded. "I got a call from a retired cop on the force two days after we came back from our Vegas trip. He said he'd been notified that my yearly gift hadn't arrived yet. That's when I knew it was dire I pass that exam and get my license back."

My mouth dropped open. "All of this has been going on behind the scenes the last two weeks and this is the first time you're speaking of it?" I shot up from the table, tears blurred my vision. "I'm so pissed at you right now, Aunt Shirley."

Old Man Jenkins chuckled dryly. "Take a number and stand in line."

"Oh, now…stop it both of you!" Aunt Shirley waved her hands in the air and scowled at me. "I didn't say anything because there's been a lot of changes for us all over the last few weeks, and I didn't want to add something else to the mix."

"Back to this Danner character," Garrett said. "When's the last time he checked in with his parole officer? Do we know?"

Aunt Shirley nodded. "My retired cop friend has been keeping tabs for me. He personally talked to Danner's parole officer yesterday. PO said Danner has been a model citizen since he was released, has always reported in or been home when PO stops by. The parole officer assured my friend he'd stop over at Danner's this Friday, even though he just saw him on Monday morning. It was the soonest he could get there. I guess the parole officer has quite a case load as it is."

"Friday!" I shrieked. "That's two more days from now!"

"So Monday was the last day we know someone saw him," Garrett said. "I'd say Los Angeles to Kansas City…that's about a twenty-hour drive. If he drove straight through, only stopping for short naps, he could very easily have gotten to Granville late last night."

"This is so not good," I said.

"No, it's not," Garrett said. "First things first, I want to speak with the person that delivered this note to you this morning."

"That would be Libby," Old Man Jenkins said. "She's the orderly that works this wing. Nice young girl. Just had a baby about four months ago."

Garrett nodded. "Okay. Can you bring Libby up here and we'll see what we can find out?"

Aunt Shirley clapped her hands together and grinned. "Let's capture us a killer!"

The three of us turned and glared at her.

Aunt Shirley threw her hands in the air. "What?"

CHAPTER 3

"Can you describe the person that gave you the note?" Garrett asked the petite brunette.

The nervous girl bit her lip and wrung her hands together. Her hazel eyes begging us not to be angry with her. "Not really. It was a man. He had on a long-sleeved shirt, pants, a hat, gloves, and sunglasses."

"Skin color?" Garrett prompted. "Did he have any markings or tattoos that you noticed?"

"He didn't have a lot of skin showing, but I think he was white. I didn't notice any tattoos." She turned and looked pleadingly at Old Man Jenkins. "I'm so sorry, Mr. Jenkins. I hope I didn't do anything wrong. He stopped at the front desk and asked me for Mrs. Jenkins's room number, but I—"

"I'm not Mrs. Jenkins!" Aunt Shirley exclaimed. "I'm still Shirley Andrews. I didn't take the old coot's name."

Libby's face turned red and she looked like she was about to burst into tears.

"It's okay, Libby," Old Man Jenkins soothed, giving Aunt Shirley an evil eye. "You actually did everything right. You should never give out residents' room numbers to strangers."

Libby nodded emphatically. "I know. And at first, he seemed okay with my response. But then when he asked again, and I gave him the same answer, he really got upset!"

"What did he do?" Garrett asked.

"He just leaned in really close and told me if I didn't give him the number, I'd come to regret it."

"You poor girl," Aunt Shirley said, trying to play nice since Old Man Jenkins had given her a warning glare. "You must have stood your ground because he didn't get up here."

Libby looked at the ground and shrugged. "Well, I told him I was really sorry and that he could stop back by in half an hour and talk with Lucy Stevenson, the executive director."

"So he came by twice this morning?" Garrett asked.

Libby nodded. "Yes. The second time he came back Ms. Stevenson was on the clock. I called her over immediately when I saw him walk through the door again."

Lucy Stevenson and I didn't always see eye to eye on things. In fact, the last time she kicked Aunt Shirley out and made me take Aunt Shirley home with me, I almost strangled the woman myself. She was a condescending know-it-all...Lucy, not Aunt Shirley.

"Well, if anyone could block his way in, it would be Lucy," I said. "The woman is a viper."

Libby let out a giggle then caught herself. "Yes, ma'am. When the gentleman tried his threats on her, she pretty much told him it would be over her dead body before he got Ms. Andrews's apartment number." She shivered. "He was really angry. I could tell. He threw the note on the counter and said it needed to be delivered immediately."

"Did he get in a car when he left?" Garret asked.

Libby shook her head. "I'm so sorry, I don't know. I was just so glad he'd finally left. I didn't pay attention if he left in a car or truck or what."

Garrett's cool features weren't fooling me. I could tell he was frustrated beyond belief.

"Thank you, Libby, for your time," Garrett said as he walked Libby to the apartment door. "If you remember something, anything at all, please give the police department a call."

"I sure will, Chief."

Garrett closed the door and sauntered over to where we were still sitting at the table.

"Do you think Lucy Stevenson will have anything more to add?" Old Man Jenkins asked.

Garrett nodded. "I'm going to talk with her next. I'll find her on my way out. Hopefully she paid better attention."

I gave Garrett my best apologetic, loving look before turning to Aunt Shirley. "I think you guys should come stay with Garrett and me out at the country house."

Aunt Shirley snorted. "The day I need to come hide out at your house for protection is the day you need to take me out back and shoot me."

I rolled my eyes at her. "I'm just worried about your safety."

"We'll be fine," Aunt Shirley insisted.

"Tell you what," Old Man Jenkins said, "if Danner comes back or anything else major happens, we'll come stay with you."

Aunt Shirley opened her mouth to argue, but Old Man Jenkins stared her down.

Aunt Shirley huffed and crossed her arms over her sagging chest.

But she didn't argue.

"I'm going to head back to the office after I talk with Lucy," Garrett said, "and see if I can't get a current photo of Danner."

I walked Garrett to the door and kissed him goodbye.

He wrapped his arms around me and nuzzled my neck. "Do me a favor, Sin. The next time you invite your aunt to come stay with us, give me a little more warning."

I grinned. "No way. Then you'll think of a way to weasel out of it!"

He kissed me again quickly on the lips. "Count on it."

***

"I have to check in at the paper," I told Aunt Shirley and Old Man Jenkins a little while later. I'd wanted to stay long enough to make sure everything was okay before heading out to get my day

23

started. "I have the town meeting article to finish up. And then Mom texted me last night and asked if I'd pick up something for the wedding at Quilter's Paradise while I was out today. Do you want to go with me, Aunt Shirley?"

Aunt Shirley crinkled her nose. "You run by the newspaper office. I'm not really feeling up to it. When you're done there, swing back by and get me and I'll go with you to Quilter's Paradise and then out to your Mom's house."

I gave each of them a hug goodbye and headed to the elevator. Aunt Shirley used to live on the third floor of the Tropical Paradise wing, but now she's residing on the second floor of the Golden Sands wing. I really had no reason to take the elevator…other than I was being lazy.

The elevator dropped me off in the expansive lobby of the Manor where residents could play chess or checkers, read by the fireplace, or just hang out and chat on the sofas.

I waved to a couple of the residents playing checkers and two of the orderlies behind the information desk. Lucy Stevenson was also there. Garrett's questions must not have taken very long.

I hopped in the Falcon and let the engine purr for a moment before I pulled out of the visitor's parking area of the Manor and headed toward the office. When I'd told Hank I needed to cut back a few hours this week because I had to get ready for the wedding, he did his normal cursing and grumbling at me.

My boss, Hank Perkins, was a retired Marine who still walked the walk and talked the talk. Once a Marine, always a Marine. Oorah! While his wife, Mindy, was the complete opposite. I don't know how it worked, but they've been happily married for years.

Mindy was sitting behind her desk flipping through a magazine when I walk into the office a few minutes later. Just my luck she called out a greeting loud enough to bring Hank out of his office.

24

"About time you were checking in," Hank grumbled around his signature unlit cigar as he leaned on his doorframe. "It's like you think you can make your own hours."

I rolled my eyes at him. "I'm getting ready to turn in a couple articles right now, so back off. I had to stop off at Aunt Shirley's this morning."

"Where is the old bat, anyway?"

"Hank!" Mindy admonished good-naturedly. "You be nice."

I wasn't exactly sure what all I should tell Hank and Mindy. After all, Garrett hadn't said I couldn't tell anyone, and since Aunt Shirley technically worked for the *Granville Gazette,* Hank should probably know.

I quickly filled them in on the morning's activities.

When I was finished, Hank let out a whistle. "That's pretty serious."

"I know," I said grimly. "I tried to get them both to stay out at Garrett's with us for the next few days but Aunt Shirley refused."

Hank grinned. "I'm sure she did." He instantly turned sober. "But she needs to watch her back. This isn't a joking matter."

"Agreed." I took the hot tea Mindy offered me and went to sit down behind my desk. "What all do you have for me before the wedding Saturday?"

"I need you to go out to the local pumpkin patch and do a feel-good piece," Hank said. "I need it by tomorrow evening."

"Got it. Anything else?"

Hank snorted. "Between your wedding in a couple days and now Aunt Shirley's drama, I think that should be enough to keep you busy." Hank shook his head and grimaced. "What the heck is Garrett thinking getting shackled to you and all your drama?" Without another word he hoisted himself off the doorframe, stepped backward into his office, and slammed his door shut.

"Thanks for the marriage counseling!" I yelled out. "Good thing we aren't paying you for your expertise!"

I still couldn't believe that Hank was officiating my wedding. What had started out as a joke recently between Garrett and Hank one night over drinks and military comradery...ended up with Hank signed up with a church recognized by the state of Missouri to ordain marriages.

Marriage advice from Mindy I'd take...Hank, no way!

When I didn't get a response from Hank, I went back to work on the computer to finish writing my piece on the latest town council meeting and the other two stories I still had out. By the time I finished, it was nearing noon. I figured Aunt Shirley would be in the mood for a fountain drink from Burger Barn before we went to the fabric store. She loved the soda dispenser at Burger Barn...they had ten different flavors you could add to your drink. For Aunt Shirley, it was like being a kid in a candy shop.

"You two be careful now, you hear?" Mindy said as I picked my keys up to leave.

"We will. Are you coming over to Mom's sometime this week to hang out and finish up last minute wedding stuff?"

"Wouldn't miss it for the world."

I blew her a kiss and hurried to the door. "I'll text you and let you know what's going on the next few days."

Granville has a population of just over ten thousand. At least, that's what the sign outside the city limits claims. I've not known that number to change much in the twenty-nine years I've been alive.

The town is made up of two main streets, Elm Street and Pike Street. They meet in the heart of downtown at a four-way stop. On the downtown square we have the courthouse, Legends Salon and Nails, a couple of banks, Steve's Sub Shop, two café-type restaurants, and a handful of antiques stores. On the outskirts of town going west, we have Burger Barn, the elementary, middle, and high schools, along with a small hospital. On the east side of town we have a small family-run grocery store, the police station, and the newspaper building where I work. Thrown into this mixture are numerous houses and churches.

When I stay at my place in town, it only takes me about three minutes to get to work. But now that I'm staying most nights out at the country house, I need to give myself about ten minutes. Still, a ten-minute commute isn't bad.

I pulled into an empty parking space at the Manor and jogged inside. I called out to a couple of the residents I knew as I scurried to the elevator. Telling myself I'd start taking the stairs next week, I hurried inside the elevator.

I gave the secret knock on Old Man Jenkins's door and was stunned to hear Aunt Shirley holler out for me to come in. I opened the door and gave her my best evil eye.

"Are you insane?" I threw my purse on the kitchen table and sank into a chair. "You can't leave the door unlocked when you know a killer is stalking you!"

"I can if I have this handy!" Aunt Shirley lifted her archaic, brown, snub-nosed revolver off the counter. "The choice of every good private investigator."

I suppressed a shudder at the thought of Aunt Shirley being a licensed private investigator again. Now she *felt* it was her duty to carry a weapon with her at all times.

"You carrying yours?" Aunt Shirley asked.

"No," I said incredulously. "I have to go to Mom's house still today. She'd *kill* me if I brought a weapon into her home."

Aunt Shirley shrugged. "I do it all the time. She just doesn't know."

"Where's your hubby?" I figured if we didn't change the subject soon, Aunt Shirley would make me carry her nunchucks or ninja stars around this afternoon for protection.

Aunt Shirley narrowed her eyes at me. "Don't you call that lying cur dog my husband. He's a no-good mangy fopdoodle!"

"Fopdoodle?" I laughed.

Aunt Shirley shook her head in disgust at me. "Yeah, fopdoodle. It means foolish man. Geez, don't they teach you young people anything in schools nowadays?"

I laughed. "I guess not. And I haven't really been in school for a while, Aunt Shirley."

"Maybe you need to go back...see if you can't learn something."

I sighed. "Are you ready to go to the fabric store before we head over to see Mom?"

"Just waiting on you. The old man is swimming down at the pool. He knows I'm leaving with you."

Aunt Shirley picked the gun up off the counter and shoved it down the waistband of her pants.

"Um...maybe you shouldn't do that," I said slowly. "You know, since you're wearing *elastic*!"

Aunt Shirley rolled her eyes. "Fine. I'll put it in my purse."

"You're gonna leave it in the Falcon when we run into the store."

"Geez, Hank's right. You really are a Shirley Temple!"

Grumbling, I shoved her out the door and down to the elevator. I figured the faster I got done at the fabric store the faster

I could pawn her off on Mom. We walked out of the Manor, waving at the girls working the information desk.

CHAPTER 4

"It's so good to see you," Blair said as Aunt Shirley and I placed our purchases on the counter.

Blair Watkins was the owner of Quilter's Paradise, a fabric and craft store recently opened in Granville. Unfortunately, her grand opening was anything but perfect when one of her store employees was murdered. Aunt Shirley and I came to the rescue and helped solve the case and in return, Blair made my wedding veil for free.

"Yes," Willa echoed woodenly, "we're so glad to see you."

Willa Trindle was not happy to see me, and she and I both knew it. Willa and I grew up attending the same church and graduated in the same class. She made my life growing up a living hell. Both her and her mom. When Aunt Shirley and I were solving the store murder, Willa came up on our radar as a possible suspect, and Willa and her mom have made sure we've never lived that slight down.

"How's your momma doing?" Aunt Shirley asked.

Willa's eyes grew wide but she let none of her sudden anger slip in front of Blair. "Fine. Just fine. In fact, she's dating someone now." Willa turned to me. "She plans on bringing him to your wedding reception. You don't mind, do you?"

Now it was my turn to bite my tongue and not give in to the anger. She and I both knew I didn't want her or her mom anywhere near my big day. But church etiquette and mid-western hospitality dictated I had to at least invite them to the reception if I didn't invite them to the actual wedding. Or at least that's what Mom said I had to do.

"Of course I don't," I lied. "Why, Garrett and I are just so honored at the outpouring of friends who have RSVP'd they're coming."

At this rate, if I tell one more lie, I'm gonna go straight to hell!

Anyone who knew Garrett knew the last thing he wanted was a large wedding or wedding reception. He was doing all of this for my mom. It was what *she* wanted, and since Mom didn't get a big wedding with Matt and Paige, Garrett thought the least we could do is meet Mom halfway.

"Tristan and I are still dating," Willa suddenly announced with glee. "So we plan on making it to your reception, too. That's still cool, right?"

My nostrils flared. I was pretty sure it was the only emotional tell I gave away on the outside, even though inside I was raging. Willa knew I had always had a maddening crush on Tristan Rainer all through high school. He was the star quarterback, popular, and never knew I existed. When Willa recently told me they were dating, it was all I could do not to rip her hair out. Not that I still wanted Tristan…I just didn't want him at my wedding.

"Of course," I said through gritted teeth and a big fake smile. "The more the merrier on my happy day."

Blair clapped her hands in glee. "Oh, Ryli, I can't wait to see you in your dress and veil." She looked over her busy store. "Well, I better get back to work. I'll see you in a couple days if not before."

Blair gave us a wave and headed toward the back of the store, leaving Aunt Shirley and me alone with the barracuda.

All of our fake smiles dropped from our faces the minute Blair walked away.

"Who's this new guy your mom has taken up with?" Aunt Shirley asked. "I haven't heard of her dating a guy."

Willa shrugged. "He's new in town. You probably don't know him."

Marveling at the fact anyone would want to date Willa's mom, I said nothing as Willa finished ringing up the items. Aunt Shirley did me a solid and paid for the last-minute wedding items. I lifted the bag by its handles and carried it outside, not bothering with anymore pleasantries none of us were feeling.

Aunt Shirley put her hand on my arm when I was about ten feet from the Falcon. Without saying a word, she pointed to the windshield then looked around. I leaned forward and squinted at what looked to be a picture under the windshield wiper.

Aunt Shirley dug into her purse and brought out her gun.

"I thought I told you to leave that in the car!" I hissed.

"I'd say it's a darn good thing I brought it." Aunt Shirley turned sideways, looking but not actively aiming the gun. Thank goodness. I didn't think Blair would like for us to scare off her customers.

"I want you to move slowly forward," Aunt Shirley directed. "Let's see what he left us."

My heart was beating double time, and I couldn't seem to make my legs move. I was about to mention my immobilization when Aunt Shirley gave me a forceful shove in my back, practically sending me sprawling on the pavement.

"What the heck, Aunt Shirley!" I straightened and glared at her. "I don't want road rash on my body three days before my wedding!"

"If you don't start doing what I say, you might not survive to attend your wedding."

My eyes widened at that realization, and I wondered for about the eightieth time why it was I couldn't seem to lead a normal life. Oh, that's right, I'm friends with Aunt Shirley.

I gingerly tiptoed over to the driver's side of the Falcon and lifted the picture from under the windshield wiper. Aunt Shirley shoved her revolver back inside her purse and snatched the photo out of my hand.

Which was perfectly fine…seeing as how I seemed frozen in place once again. The photo had terrified me so badly, I thought I was gonna pee myself.

"Well, if this doesn't beat all," Aunt Shirley muttered.

It was a photo of Aunt Shirley and me walking out of the Manor not even thirty minutes ago.

"I'm really freaked," I whispered. "Should we call Garrett?"

Aunt Shirley shook her head. "Not much he's gonna be able to do right now. We know Danner is in town, and Blair doesn't need the police here at the store on something not related to her or the store. Let's just get in the car and go to your mom's house like we planned."

Tears filled my eyes. "I don't *want* to go to Mom's if he's following us. My gosh, not only is Mom there, but so is Paige!"

"Ryli, this is a small town. If he wanted to know where your mom lived, all he'd have to do is ask around. With the wedding in a few days, no one is gonna think twice about a stranger asking where your mom's house is. He could just be a lost out-of-town guest for all they know."

That thought had me bent over like I'd been sucker punched.

"Let's go," Aunt Shirley said. "Get in the Falcon and drive over to your mom's. She's expecting us, and we aren't going to give her any reason to worry. It's going to be hard enough explaining this to her calmly and rationally."

***

"I can't *believe* this!" Mom said for the tenth time in ten minutes. "I don't know if I want to take you both over my knee, give you both a hug, or throttle you both!"

I thought Mom was taking the news of Aunt Shirley's stalker pretty well, all things considered.

"Oh, Ryli." My best friend and twin-carrying sister-in-law, Paige, rubbed her enormous belly and gave me a sympathetic smile. "And here I thought we'd get through this week unscathed."

"This is *really* bad." Mom stopped rearranging the wedding gifts that had been coming nonstop to her house for the past two days and gave me a hard look. "Does Garrett think we should postpone the wedding?"

"No!" I cried, almost spilling the spiked hot tea I was drinking. "He says everything is under control. We are to go about our day like normal and let him take care of it."

I added that last part for Aunt Shirley. I knew she was itching to go look for Danner on her own…with me in tow.

My cell phone vibrated, alerting me to a text. I opened it and frowned.

34

"It's Garrett. He said he's been trying to reach someone in the parole department out in California that he can talk to about what happened, but so far he's only been told he'd get a call back. He said he might be a little late for dinner tonight, but he'd be here as soon as he could."

Mom was having one last small gathering at her house for dinner before the wedding. The rehearsal dinner was going to be just finger foods, so Mom wanted one last intimate gathering before the wedding with Paige and Matt, Mindy and Hank, Aunt Shirley and Old Man Jenkins, as well as Mom's boyfriend, Doc Powell.

I watched with shock and horror as Mom went over to the stove to pour a mug of hot tea…and added a splash of booze. Mom was not a tea and booze drinker. She must *really* be upset.

"I think we should all stick together," Mom said after taking a large gulp of her spiked tea. "Ryli, I want you, Garrett, Aunt Shirley, and Waylon to stay in town at my place. I have plenty of room, and we can work on last-minute wedding preparations. Paige and Matt can stay in their house, and when Matt's at work, Paige can stay here with us."

Aunt Shirley shook her head. "Ain't happening, Janine. I know you mean well, but Waylon and I are fine where we are."

"How do you know?" Mom shot back angrily. "Just because this crazy psycho didn't know your apartment number this morning doesn't mean he can't learn it between now and before he's arrested."

My brows shot up at Mom's anger. Usually she was the cool head in the group.

"She's right, Aunt Shirley," I said. "Maybe you should think again about our offer."

"I'll tell you what," Aunt Shirley said. "If something else major happens tomorrow, Waylon and I will come stay with one of you."

"Something else major?" Mom growled. "Like what? One of you dying?"

My mouth dropped open. "I don't think that'll happen." I recognized the fear in my voice but hoped no one else did.

"Simmer down, Janine," Aunt Shirley said. "No one is going to die this week."

If only Aunt Shirley would have been right.

CHAPTER 5

"I thought last night went pretty well, all things considered." Garrett finished latching his gun belt before turning to me. "I mean, your mom looks like she needs a long vacation, but she managed to pull off a great dinner without killing Aunt Shirley."

"Small wonder."

Garrett smiled and leaned over the bed to give me a kiss. "What's on your agenda today?"

I sighed and threw back the covers. "I'm going to go get Aunt Shirley and meet Mom, Paige, and Mindy at Legends Salon and Nails to get our fingers and toes done for the wedding. Then afterward I need to help Mom start setting up tables in the backyard. Around four I'm heading out to the pumpkin farm to take pictures. School will be out by then so I can get some pictures real quick with some kids. What about you?"

"I'm going to hit all the local campsites I know of, see if anyone has seen someone matching Danner's description. Granville may not be that large, but there are a lot of places Danner could hide. I have Officer Ryan on phone duty. I told him I didn't care if he was calling every half an hour. I'm going to talk to someone today down at the parole office in Los Angeles if it's the last thing I do. Matt's staying in town, going into businesses, chatting up people. See if anyone has noticed someone new in town. Don't forget to take the photo of Danner I printed out for you. And please be aware of your surroundings at all times today."

"I will. Be safe."

"Back at ya, Sin."

He gave me one more kiss before leaving, and I ogled his backside as he walked out the bedroom door.

I waited until almost nine to go round up Aunt Shirley for our appointment at Legends. Mainly because I didn't want to spend any more time in the salon than I had to. The former owner, Iris Newman, was murdered almost one year ago to the day. I'd only been to the salon a couple times since then, preferring to drive to Brywood to get my hair done. It was still too creepy going into Iris's old shop.

Plus, the new owner, Daphne Dowerson, was a little too strange for my taste in a hairdresser. Eclectic, mid-thirties woman with multi-colored hair, piercings in her ears and nose, and colorful tattoos lining her arms. Aunt Shirley loved getting her hair done by Daphne. Me, I wasn't so brave.

I parked the Falcon on the side of the street a block away from Legends. Mom's SUV was already parked in front of the salon, so Aunt Shirley and I hustled inside. Luckily it was a slow Thursday morning, with Mom, Paige, Mindy, Aunt Shirley, and me taking up the whole salon.

"Shirley!" Daphne exclaimed when she saw Aunt Shirley hurry through the doors. "Your hair looks fabulous this morning."

Aunt Shirley gave her multi-colored bouffant a pat. "Thanks, Daph. Still loving it!"

Mom sent me a quiet, knowing look. I looked away so I wouldn't laugh out loud. I didn't want to hurt anyone's feelings.

"Right this way, ladies." Daphne said, motioning for us to follow her through the side doorway that led to a tiny, spa-like room. There were four manicure tables and four pedicure chairs crammed in the small room. "I've asked Cindy Troyer and Brandy Thompson to come in a little early today so they can start on the toes while I do the nails. Is that okay with you girls?"

"Sounds great," Mom said.

"Two things," Daphne said. "One, I need Ryli to pick out the color she wants everyone to wear for the wedding. And two, who wants champagne?"

I perked up at that question. I vaguely recalled that Legends was now serving wine and champagne with your hair and nail appointment. Pretty classy for a small-town salon. Everyone but Paige lifted a hand.

"I'll just have a water," Paige sulked.

I patted her on the arm. "Once these babies break out, I promise to treat you to a night you won't forget."

"I'm holding you to that."

As Daphne passed the champagne around and I picked out a matching color for everyone, Cindy and Brandy walked into the room and started turning on the water for the foot massagers. Daphne took Mom to start on her nails and the rest of us sat down in the vibrating chairs. I sat back and enjoyed the attention.

"Ladies," Cindy sang as she started working on Paige's toes. "Have you guys heard about the new guy in town?"

My eyes flew open and I sat up in the chair. "What new guy?"

Had Cindy come across Danner somehow?

"I don't know his name, but evidentially he's seeing Phoebe Trindle! Can you believe that? I hear they've been seeing each other for a few weeks now."

I groaned. "Willa made a big deal about bringing him to my reception Saturday night. She didn't tell me his name, just that her mom was seeing someone."

Cindy scrunched her nose. "What kind of guy would knowingly date a vicious woman like Phoebe Trindle?"

"Maybe he doesn't know how horrible she is," Mindy suggested.

"Shouldn't take him long to find out," Paige said.

"How about any other new men?" I asked as casually as I could. "Have you heard or seen a guy you didn't immediately recognize?"

"You looking for another man, Ryli?" Cindy teased.

I laughed. "No. I'm happy with the one I have. I was just wondering if anyone has mentioned to you guys about seeing another stranger in town."

Daphne furrowed her brow. "Not that I'm aware of."

Cindy Troyer shook her head. "I haven't heard of anyone else new in town. Why?"

"Oh, no reason," I nonchalantly replied. "I just thought I saw someone in town the other day I didn't recognize."

"Maybe it's the new guy that's seeing Phoebe Trindle," Brandy laughed. "What did he look like?"

I thought back to the current photo Garrett had given me this morning. "Salt and pepper hair, hard eyes—I mean brown eyes, medium build."

"That's definitely not Phoebe Trindle's new guy," Brandy said as she applied a coat of polish to Paige's toes. "He was tall and skinny. Looked like a strong gust of wind would knock him over."

40

"Granville's a small town," Daphne said as she motioned for Mom to sit in a pedicure chair and for Mindy to sit at the table to get her fingernails done. "But I'm sure there are new people moving here all the time."

Figuring she was right, I slouched back down in the vibrating chair and took a sip of my champagne, patiently waiting my turn.

"So, are you and Aunt Shirley doing a co-honeymoon thing?" Daphne asked twenty minutes later when she started on my nails.

"No!" I exclaimed. "Everyone keeps asking me that, but it's not happening."

Aunt Shirley cackled from her pedicure chair and slapped her knee. "You never know. We just may."

I shook my head emphatically at Daphne. "No. We're not."

Two and a half hours later, fingers and toes looking amazing, the five of us walked out of Legends feeling relaxed and pampered.

"What now?" Aunt Shirley asked.

I looked at my watch. "It's a little after eleven-thirty. How about I swing by the Burger Barn, pick us all up some lunch, then take it back to Mom's to eat?"

"Sounds good," Mom said. "Meet you back at the house around noon."

With a wave, Aunt Shirley and I crossed over to the Falcon and got inside.

As I started toward Burger Barn, Aunt Shirley dug out her cell phone. "I just wanna call the old man real quick and make sure he's going to the cafeteria for lunch."

I heard the ringing on the other end through Aunt Shirley's phone. After four rings, it went straight through to Old Man

Jenkins's voicemail. "Darn that man! He probably doesn't have his hearing aide in. Let's stop by so I can double check on him."

I wisely kept my mouth shut and didn't tease her about the fact she was checking up on him like a good wife should do. I was pretty sure that would get me slapped upside the head.

Still grumbling to herself, I parked the Falcon outside the Manor and Aunt Shirley pushed open her door.

"Wait," I said. "I'll go up with you."

Aunt Shirley scowled at me. "Why? It won't take but a minute."

"I don't know. Ever since Danner sent that picture of us outside the Manor, I'm kinda spooked."

Aunt Shirley rolled her eyes. "C'mon, ya big sissy. Let's go."

I pushed the front door to the Manor open and automatically went to wave to Lucy Stevenson behind the information desk. Only it wasn't Lucy behind the desk this afternoon.

We took the elevator up to the second floor and made our way to Aunt Shirley's apartment door. My breath caught when I noticed the front door was ajar. No way would Old Man Jenkins leave it that way.

Aunt Shirley quickly dug in her purse and yanked out her gun. Dropping her purse to the floor she motioned me back. "Stick close. Do everything I tell you to do."

"Shouldn't we call Garrett?" I whispered.

Aunt Shirley swept her eyes over me. "You got your phone on you?"

I stifled a groan when I realized I'd left my phone inside my purse…which was in the car. "No. Maybe we should go downstairs and have someone call the police."

"Ryli, I need you to pull yourself together. I'm going in. My husband could be inside dead for all I know."

Tears filled my eyes and my heart pinged at the thought of Old Man Jenkins lying inside dead. But I knew I had to be strong for Aunt Shirley. "Okay. I got this."

Aunt Shirley nodded her head then slowly pushed the front door the rest of the way open…scanning first right and then left. Tiptoeing farther inside, she motioned me with her head to follow her. Gun held tightly in her grip, Aunt Shirley proceeded to creep around the sofa, eyes still on the open doorway leading to the bedroom.

"There's something on the dining room table," Aunt Shirley whispered. "I'm going to cover the doorway, and I want you to walk nice and slow to the table."

Crap! Why wasn't I the one carrying the gun so she'd have to do that?

Ignoring the tremble in my legs, I slowly shuffled to the dining room table. Sitting on the table was a small pumpkin with a knife sticking out of its top. A note was sitting next to it. I glanced back and saw Aunt Shirley, gun and eyes glued to the doorway. Her fierce gaze should have brought relief, but my fear was too great.

I was about to reach out and pick up the note when movement by the front door caught my eye. Without thinking, I let out a blood-curdling scream.

CHAPTER 6

"What the heck?" Old Man Jenkins shouted as he stumbled back into the door jamb, clutching his heart.

"Dang it, Waylon!" Aunt Shirley growled, lowering her gun and her shoulders. "What's the big idea?"

"Me?" he shouted. "What about you? What are you doing pointing your gun at me?"

For the first time I took in Old Man Jenkins's attire. He was dressed in his bright yellow Speedo, beach towel slung over one shoulder.

Relief flooded through me and I let out a giggle. I plopped down in one of the dining chairs and just let the waves of emotion wash over me. I hadn't been this scared in a long time. The thought that something awful might have happened to Old Man Jenkins *just* as I was getting to know him left me shaken beyond belief.

"So let me ask again, woman…what's the big idea?"

I outright laughed at that statement. No way was Aunt Shirley gonna hold back now.

When I didn't hear cursing from Aunt Shirley, I looked up. Her face was ashen and she was visibly shaking. I jumped up to help her into a chair but she held me off with her hand. "If I weren't so relieved you're alive, I'd kill you with my bare hands right now."

Old Man Jenkins shut the door and moved slowly toward Aunt Shirley. "I can see that. What's going on, Shirley? Has something happened?"

Aunt Shirley wiped a hand across her aging face, surreptitiously trying to brush away the tear that had started to fall. "Yes, something has happened. I came here today to see if you wanted lunch, and when I arrived at the door it was ajar. When I went in, I could—"

"Why on *Earth* would you put yourself and Ryli in danger and enter if you thought someone was in here?" Old Man Jenkins shouted.

"I thought you might be hurt," Aunt Shirley whispered.

"I don't care! You don't risk your life for me! Hell, you don't even *like* me right now, remember?"

Aunt Shirley wiped at her eyes again. "Just shut up for a minute, Waylon. I can't think straight when you're yelling at me."

I watched the two banter back and forth with each other. If the circumstances hadn't been so dire, I'd have enjoyed the show. I looked down and remembered the pumpkin and note.

"Want me to read the note?" I asked.

"What note?" Old Man Jenkins asked.

I didn't say anything, just pointed to the note on the table.

"Read it," Aunt Shirley demanded.

"It says, 'Don't you think it's time we *bury* the hatchet? D.'"

Old Man Jenkins swore. "And I suppose Danner left the pumpkin with the knife sticking out of it?"

I nodded. I was too busy suffering from my own flashbacks to answer. Last year around this time someone had left *me* a carved pumpkin on my front porch with a present inside—a human tongue.

"I'm calling Garrett," Old Man Jenkins said as he went into the kitchen and grabbed his cell phone off the counter.

"Fine," Aunt Shirley snapped. "Then go put some pants on before he gets here!"

Ten minutes later, Garrett came storming through the front door. I was surprised it had taken him this long to respond.

"I was out at one of the campgrounds when I got Jenkins's call," Garrett said as if reading my mind. He leaned in and gave me a soft kiss on my lips. Wanting to feel his arms around me, I sagged against him. "Shhh." He gathered me close and kissed the side of my temple. "I got you. Everything is fine."

"Nothing is gonna be fine until this psycho is captured," I whispered.

"Let me process the scene and then we'll talk."

Garrett radioed in to the station that he'd arrived, and then called Matt for backup. By the time Matt arrived, Garrett had finished questioning a fully dressed Old Man Jenkins and Aunt Shirley.

"I'm pretty sure we won't get fingerprints," Garrett said as he slid the note in a plastic baggie. "But just in case."

"How you holding up, Sis?" Matt asked as he gave me a hug.

"Pretty shaken up. I won't lie."

"I don't like the fact this man knows where we live," Old Man Jenkins said. "How did that happen?"

"I can't imagine anyone here gave out the apartment number," Garrett said. "Especially after I spoke to the ladies behind the counter yesterday. They knew how important it was *not* to give out apartment numbers."

Aunt Shirley waved her hand in the air. "It's like I told Ryli today, with the wedding in a couple days, a lot of the townspeople wouldn't think it odd a stranger's in town asking about where we all live."

Matt frowned. "I need someone to stay with Paige when I'm not home."

"I'm on it," Garrett said. "That means you two are staying either out at our house in the country or with Ryli's mom. We are to stay together as much as possible."

When Aunt Shirley opened her mouth to argue, Garrett raised his hand. "I will not be argued with on this matter. This is a crime scene, and I'm treating it like one. You are to get your things and get out."

"Fine," Aunt Shirley huffed. "But I don't want to stay out in the country away from the action. We'll stay in town as long as we stay at Ryli's cottage house."

I looked at Garrett to gauge his reaction. "I can get Officer Ryan to stay at Janine's place with Paige when Matt or I can't be there." Garrett turned to Aunt Shirley. "I can't believe I'm doing this, but now that you are a licensed PI, I can legally employ you as a consultant for the police department. I'm entrusting you to make sure you, Jenkins, and Ryli stay put tonight at Ryli's house in town."

The surprised look on Aunt Shirley's face said it all. "Of course. You can count on me."

"Good. Matt, let's get this evidence tagged and sent off. Ryli, I'll call you later if I hear anything. What's left for you to do today?"

"I was supposed to go to the pumpkin patch around four to get pictures. Think I can still do that?"

Garrett looked pointedly at Aunt Shirley and Old Man Jenkins. "I assume you both will be packing?"

They nodded solemnly.

"Then I think it'll be safe," Garrett said.

Garrett and Matt left a few minutes later and Aunt Shirley and Old Man Jenkins went to pack their belongings.

"Make sure you pack both your guns," Aunt Shirley said as they both headed down the hallway.

"Don't you worry yourself about me," Old Man Jenkins grumbled. "I got it all under control."

"I'm the one that's consulting with the police, old man. You take orders from me now."

Their bickering died off as they entered the bedroom. Breathing a sigh of relief, I sat down on the couch and basked in the quiet. How in the world was I going to take those two living with me until Danner could be found?

"Aunt Shirley," I yelled down the hallway, "can I call Mom from your phone so she knows why we're late? I'm sure she's been hounding me on my cell phone."

"Sure thing, honey. Tell her we should be there in about twenty minutes. We still need to go by and get lunch."

To say Mom was upset is putting it mildly, but at this stage of the game, she wasn't totally surprised. With a promise we'd be careful, I assured her we'd be there in about twenty minutes with lunch.

Five minutes later Old Man Jenkins came out of the back room carrying a duffle bag and muttering to himself about silly old women.

Fifteen minutes later Aunt Shirley finally came out of the back bedroom carrying two suitcases…one housing clothes, the other makeup. I knew this routine like the back of my hand.

"You'll only be gone a few days," I admonished. "What all did you pack?"

"I packed like I was on a case. I have an outfit for every occasion we may come across."

I rolled my eyes but said nothing. There was no arguing with crazy.

As we finally piled into the elevator, I whispered another prayer that I would be able to get through this rough patch and marry Garrett without this cloud hanging over us. When the elevator doors slid open, I wheeled one of Aunt Shirley's bags behind me and followed them out toward the lobby.

I went to wave at Lucy behind the desk, only to realize once again she wasn't there. She hadn't been there four hours ago…and she wasn't there now. As Old Man Jenkins went to tell some of his cronies goodbye, I wandered over to the information desk.

"I haven't seen Lucy this morning," I said to the young orderly behind the desk.

He gave me the once-over before assuming the bored look again. "She called in sick this morning. Said she had a cold."

I furrowed my brow. "She looked okay to me yesterday."

The orderly shrugged. "I don't know. She sounded weird, though."

"Weird, how?" I asked.

The man huffed like I was keeping him from something important. "Like her speech was slow. She was taking shallow breaths." He gave me a cocky grin. "Like she was afraid she was going to hurl. She said under no circumstance was she to be called on the phone or bothered in any way today."

Warning bells went off. "Did Chief Kimble come talk to you today?"

The young man's eyes widened. "No. I actually just got back to the desk. I had a couple things I had to take care of."

When the cat's away the mice will play.

I thanked him then turned to walk toward Aunt Shirley and Old Man Jenkins. I motioned Aunt Shirley over. "Lucy called in today, said she was sick."

"Okay."

I gave her my best exasperated look. "Am I the only one here who thinks it odd that the very morning she calls in sick is the same day Danner finds out where you live?"

Aunt Shirley's face went white. "Oh, crap. You're right. I say we go out to her place and see what's going on."

"I think we should call Garrett," I said.

Aunt Shirley held up her hand. "First off, I'm officially on consult now. That means you don't have to go running to Garrett all the time at the drop of a hat."

I narrowed my eyes at her. "I don't go running to Garrett."

"You do. And second, this could be nothing. No sense wasting Garrett's time over a coincidence."

50

I leveled my gaze at her. "You don't believe in coincidences."

"I'll get the old man," Aunt Shirley said, ignoring my statement. "He'll know where Lucy lives seeing as how he worked at the post office all those years."

Which is *exactly* how we got in trouble last year. Back then, I was certain Patty Carter was the murderer, and when Aunt Shirley arm-twisted Old Man Jenkins into spilling his guts on where she lived, we hightailed it out to her place to confront her.

I was wrong then…was I wrong now about Lucy?

A few minutes later Old Man Jenkins and Aunt Shirley hurried over to where I was pacing. Still uncertain of whether or not I should call Garrett, I filled Old Man Jenkins in about my theory.

"We need to call Garrett," he said firmly. His no-nonsense response left no doubt he thought we were in over our heads.

Aunt Shirley hit him lightly on the arm. "Oh, Waylon, it could be nothing. I'm sure he's got better things to do than go check on a sick woman."

Old Man Jenkins scowled at Aunt Shirley. "You don't think she's sick though, do you?"

Aunt Shirley shrugged. "Who knows. I say the three of us just go out and check on her real quick. Put it to rest. You know where she lives, right?"

Old Man Jenkins hesitated before answering. "I know where she lives. Or at least where she used to live. I can't say for sure she's still there, it's been years since I worked for the post office."

"Good," Aunt Shirley beamed, ignoring his hedging. "We can be there and back to Janine's house with lunch in just a matter of minutes, I'm sure."

I bit my lip...wrestling with what I should do. "Okay. Let's do it. Hopefully you're right and Lucy really is just sick."

Aunt Shirley rubbed her hands together. "Let's roll!"

CHAPTER 7

Lucy Stevenson lived on the west side of town in a one-story brick house by the elementary school. I pulled into the driveway and cut off the Falcon's engine. Her front porch and yard were decorated with tiny bales of hay and myriad pumpkins of various sizes. A scarecrow family was staked into the ground by the bales of hay. There wasn't a single light on inside the house. Not that there needed to be of course, but it still looked eerie.

"How are we going to do this?" I asked Aunt Shirley.

Aunt Shirley pulled her snub-nose revolver from her purse.

"Jeez, woman!" Old Man Jenkins exclaimed. "Maybe we don't go in with guns blazing. You'll give Lucy a heart attack if she's just home sick."

"Maybe you should bring yours," Aunt Shirley said to Old Man Jenkins.

I heard Old Man Jenkins swear, and I wanted to join him.

"I'm not taking my gun," he said. "Especially since we believe Lucy is just in there sick."

"Should we bring in Garrett yet?" I asked.

"Give me a couple minutes," Aunt Shirley said as she slowly made her way to the front door, her head moving side to side to take in her surroundings.

Old Man Jenkins shook his head and quietly followed her...I brought up the rear.

Aunt Shirley reached out and jiggled the front door handle. Expecting it to be locked, we all sucked in a breath when the door gave way and opened a fraction of an inch.

"Call out," Old Man Jenkins said. "She could be in the bathroom or something like that. We don't want to startle her."

Aunt Shirley cleared her throat. "Lucy? It's Shirley Andrews."

"Shirley Jenkins," Old Man Jenkins muttered.

Aunt Shirley scowled at him over her shoulder before hollering even louder. "It's Shirley Andrews. Are you decent? Can we come in?"

No response.

"Let me go first," Old Man Jenkins said, trying to push past Aunt Shirley.

"Cool your jets," Aunt Shirley countered. "I'm the one with a gun. You follow *my* lead."

Old Man Jenkins's nostrils flared but he didn't say another word.

Counting to ten so I didn't scream at them both for being childish, I closed my eyes and took another deep breath. Something was going to have to give with these two before they tore each other apart limb from limb.

Aunt Shirley held her gun up in front of her and stepped across the threshold and into Lucy's house…followed once again by Old Man Jenkins and myself.

I looked around the living room but didn't see anything amiss. The house was deathly quiet. Not even the TV was blaring for background noise.

And then I heard it…the faintest sound of music coming from down the hallway.

My blood turned iced cold. I remembered what Aunt Shirley had said about Danner playing music so the neighbors didn't hear the victim's scream. Whimpering, I reached out and grabbed hold of Old Man Jenkins.

"I hear it, too," Aunt Shirley muttered. "Maybe you two should stay back while I go take a look."

"Maybe you should wait here until I go get my .38 special out of the car," Old Man Jenkins whispered, "and we do this together."

"You snooze you lose, old man," Aunt Shirley hissed. "I told you to bring it."

"Can we just *do* something?" I gritted out. "I'm tired of hearing you two bicker…and I'm really scared right now."

Old Man Jenkins patted my hand. "Sorry, Ryli. It's just how your aunt and I communicate. We'll be more mindful."

Aunt Shirley met Old Man Jenkins's eyes and motioned with her head down the hall.

Taking a deep breath, I followed the two of them down the narrow, dark hall of Lucy's home.

Please just let her be sick in bed, listening to music. Please just let her be sick in bed, listening to music.

Aunt Shirley held up a hand and we stopped in front of a closed door. I assumed it was Lucy's bedroom. Aunt Shirley motioned for us to get up against the wall out of sight while she reached out and slowly turned the bedroom door handle.

It popped open a fraction of an inch.

Aunt Shirley turned sideways and with her right shoulder pushed the door open the rest of the way then scooted into the room so fast it was a blur. I peeked in and saw her taking in the rest of the room, making sure it was clear.

I then glanced at the bed and was momentarily confused.

It was empty.

What the heck?

Music was coming through Lucy's iPod via an external speaker.

"Something's not right," Aunt Shirley whispered. "Lucy should be in here. The bedroom is where he liked to take his victims."

"Maybe she's somewhere else in the house," Old Man Jenkins suggested.

"If she's sick, maybe she's making hot tea in the kitchen," I said.

Aunt Shirley nodded. "Let's check the kitchen."

Not waiting for Aunt Shirley to take the lead, Old Man Jenkins strode down the hallway like he had on a bullet-proof vest. I could hear Aunt Shirley cursing him behind me.

"Waylon Jenkins, slow your saggy butt down right now. You don't have any protection!"

Ignoring Aunt Shirley's tirade, Old Man Jenkins continued down the hall then took a right at the archway.

I let Aunt Shirley rush past me in the hallway. I wasn't exactly eager to find Lucy—dead or alive. Dead, it would be more than I could stand. Alive, she'd probably rip us a new one for barging into her home uninvited.

56

Aunt Shirley turned around and put out her hand. "You might not want to come in."

"Why?" I peeked around her on impulse then wished I hadn't.

Lucy Stevenson was sitting at her kitchen table, blood pooled on her chest where her throat had been slashed.

I folded like a card table and put my head down by my legs. "I will *not* be sick. I will *not* be sick."

I was tired of constantly having a throw-up reaction when I saw dead bodies. If I was gonna start doing PI work with Aunt Shirley, I needed to get tougher skin. At least, that's what she's constantly telling me.

"You okay?" Aunt Shirley asked.

"I'm fine. I'm fine." I waved her off, repeating the words over and over again, more for myself than for her.

"There's a note," Old Man Jenkins said.

"What's it say?" Aunt Shirley asked.

I turned to where Old Man Jenkins was standing in the kitchen. He leaned over the table without touching anything and peered down at the note. "It says, 'I wish that just once people wouldn't act like the clichés they are—Six Feet Under.'"

"What the heck does that mean?" Aunt Shirley asked.

I shrugged. "I don't know."

Aunt Shirley sighed. "Well, Ryli...I thinking maybe you better call Garrett."

"Ya think?" I asked snarkily.

Old Man Jenkins chuckled softly. "Yeah, we think."

I dug in the pocket of my jeans and pulled out my cell phone. I'd crammed it in there instead of my purse just in case we came across a moment like this. I stood there, wondering just what I was going to say. Not that Garrett hadn't received his fair share of calls from me about finding dead bodies, that's for sure. I just hate that initial sigh of resignation he always gives me. Like my finding dead bodies is somehow his cross to bear.

"Kimble here."

The corners of my mouth lifted at his greeting. "Soon-to-be Kimble here."

"Sin. Everything okay on your end?"

I sighed then took a deep breath. "Not really. For some reason when I was leaving the Manor, it struck me as odd that Lucy Stevenson hadn't been behind the desk the two times I walked by. So I asked the orderly behind the desk about Lucy, and he said Lucy called in sick."

"Okay. Tell me you aren't calling me from inside her house?"

I hesitated only a moment. "I am. See, Aunt Shirley thought—"

"Let me stop you right there. I don't really care at this particular moment what Aunt Shirley thought."

I glanced at Aunt Shirley, wondering if she heard Garrett.

The scowl on her face told me she had.

"We brought Old Man Jenkins with us," I added lamely.

Garrett laughed bitterly. "I somehow doubt he just volunteered. It was probably more of a dragging."

I bit my lip and said nothing.

"I'm assuming she's dead?" Garrett asked.

"Yes," I whispered.

"And you've secured the area? You're sure the killer isn't around?" I could hear Garrett's desk chair squeak as he stood up.

"I'm sure." It was pretty much a lie. We hadn't secured anything.

"I'll be there in about three minutes."

"Thanks."

I hung up the phone and sighed.

"That boy needs an attitude adjustment," Aunt Shirley growled. "I don't know how you can stand the thought of being married to someone who's always grouchy."

Old Man Jenkins winked at me then turned to Aunt Shirley. "The only time that boy is grouchy is when he comes in contact with you."

I smiled weakly. Nice to know someone was on my side.

CHAPTER 8

"Ya know," Garrett said, pacing back and forth in front of Lucy's house, "I'm not even going to ask why it is you didn't call me before coming over here."

I could tell by the tic in his jaw he was pretty pissed.

"Let's just focus on what we're gonna do from here, Ace." Aunt Shirley said. "The MO may be a little different, but you and I both know this was Danner's work."

Garrett closed his eyes and counted to ten. "I hate to admit it, but I know you're right. But here's the thing...*you* aren't going to do anything. You are going to let the Granville Police Department handle it from here."

Aunt Shirley crossed her arms over her sagging chest and lifted a brow. How in the world the decrepit old woman managed to look intimidating with her ridiculously colored burgundy, purple, and orange hair blowing in the breeze was beyond me...but she did.

"I believe you hired me—"

"And I can fire you just as fast," Garrett said before Aunt Shirley could finish her sentence.

"Have you heard from the parole officer out in California yet?" I asked, hoping to defuse the tension.

Garrett sighed. "No. I keep getting the runaround. I spoke to someone about half an hour ago and they told me there was nothing to justify sending someone out to Danner's house since Danner just checked in on Monday."

"I'm gonna call my cop friend who's retired," Aunt Shirley said. "Have him go check out Danner's house. Maybe peek in some windows and see if anyone's home."

"I won't tell you no," Garrett said. "In fact, I'd appreciate it."

Aunt Shirley gave him a sly grin but said nothing.

"At least we know how Danner got our apartment number," Old Man Jenkins said. "I didn't look too long at the body, but I'd say this Danner character tortured Lucy for the information before he outright killed her."

Garrett nodded gravely. "Looks that way."

"I'm really scared," I said. "I mean, not for myself personally. But I'm scared for Mom and for Paige while Matt is at work."

"I'm thinking we contact Doc Powell and let him in on what's happened here this morning," Garrett said. "He told me yesterday if things got out of hand he'd be more than willing to close his practice for a couple days and focus on helping out."

Doc Powell's veterinary clinic was outside town a few miles. Last year when Karen had tried to poison me with Hemlock but instead poisoned Miss Molly by accident, Doc Powell was the veterinarian who'd saved Miss Molly's life. I'd forever be grateful for his help. And the fact he's been seeing my mom for about a year now makes him even more special to me.

"What about Paige?" I asked.

Garrett frowned and started pacing again. He looked over at Matt and Officer Ryan standing just inside Lucy's living room.

"Officer Ryan," Garrett called. "Can you come here a minute?"

Officer Ryan could pass for Dwayne Johnson's twin. Not only was he tall, dark, handsome, and bald…but he had muscles in places I didn't even know it was possible to have. Officer Ryan has been with the Granville Police Department not quite two years now, joining on after he left the Army.

"What's up, Chief?" His gorgeous face was stone serious…not a trace of a smile anywhere. Officer Ryan was definitely someone you didn't want to meet in a dark alley if you were a thug.

"Can you do me a favor? I need you to go to the newspaper right now and explain to Hank what's happened here. Tell him I'll call him later because I'm going to need his help."

"I can do that," I said. "I can go talk with Hank."

Garrett smiled placatingly at me. "I think it will mean a little more if Officer Ryan does it. No offense, Sin, but you and Aunt Shirley are almost always in trouble. You telling Hank you need his help won't implore him much."

I let out a breath of disgust. "I'll have you know that…" I trailed off. Who was I kidding? Garrett was right. It would be more official if Officer Ryan went to talk with Hank.

Garrett turned to Old Man Jenkins. "I'll feel safe leaving Doc Powell, Janine, and Paige in Hank's capable hands for protection. This way you, Aunt Shirley, and Ryli can stay at Ryli's place in town."

Officer Ryan gave me an open-palmed thwack on my shoulder—his idea of comfort I'm sure—before turning to go to his patrol car. A few seconds later he was gone.

62

Garrett turned to me. "Ryli, call your mom or go by her house and see if we can't meet at her place around six tonight. Hopefully that will give Aunt Shirley enough time to get ahold of her guy and hear back from him."

"I'll call him the minute we leave here," Aunt Shirley promised.

"I'll go by the sub shop tonight and pick up subs for everyone," Garrett continued. "Jenkins, you still have that .38 special, right?"

"I do," Old Man Jenkins said solemnly. "And I promise from here on out I'll carry it."

Garrett nodded at Old Man Jenkins, and I saw a look pass between the two men.

"Are we still going to be able to get married Saturday?" I asked, trying to keep the tears from pooling in my eyes.

Garrett brushed his hand across my face. "Yes. I promise you, Ryli Jo Sinclair, nothing is going to keep me from meeting you down at the end of the aisle come Saturday evening."

I swallowed hard. "And tomorrow? Do you think we can still do the wedding rehearsal? Will it be safe?"

Garrett let out a harsh laugh. "We're being married by Hank. I know for a fact the man has more guns in his possession than even I have in mine. We can have a wedding rehearsal safely on Friday, trust me."

"Okay," I said, wanting more than anything to trust what he was telling me. "What about the Manor? Has anyone told them what's happened to Lucy?"

Garrett shook his head. "I'm going to go over there as soon as everything is done here. I'm assuming Melvin Collins will be finished with the body soon."

"I should probably go out to your house and get some clothes," I said. "I don't really have anything at the house here in town. Everything's at your place."

"Actually," Garett said. "I'd rather you left me a list. I'll go out and get some things."

I nodded. "Okay. I can do that."

"Plus I'm going to bring Miss Molly in town. I don't want her there by herself."

I reached up and gave him a quick kiss on the cheek. "Thank you! I didn't want to sound crazy by asking you to bring her to me."

Garrett smiled. "I figured you'd want her close where you could keep an eye on her. Now, just go about your day like nothing has changed. I'll text you when I can."

"Please be careful." He must have sensed my need for comfort because he gathered me close to him and kissed my temple.

"It's getting a little creepy," Aunt Shirley said. "Most people don't make out at a crime scene."

I giggled, drew back, and rested my head against Garrett's chest. He kissed the top of my head. "Jealous?"

Aunt Shirley's face turned red, and I had to bite my tongue to keep from laughing again.

"Let's go, you little hussy," Aunt Shirley snapped. "We still have a lot of things to get done before the wedding rehearsal tomorrow…namely apprehend a killer."

"*We* will be doing the apprehending," Garrett said, giving Aunt Shirley a pointed look.

She shrugged. "That's what I said."

***

"I need to stop by my house in town real quick if we are staying there tonight," I said. "I haven't spent the night there in weeks. I'll need to turn the heat on."

It only took a few minutes to drive over to my little cottage. I was going to miss this house so much. The one-bedroom home had served me well in the couple years I lived there.

"I'll be right back," I said to Aunt Shirley and Old Man Jenkins.

I made my way up the sagging porch and unlocked the door. I was about to step inside when I heard someone calling my name.

"Ryli," Miss Mabel yelled over from her yard. "Dear, is that you?"

"Yes, Miss Mabel."

I watched as my ninety-year-old neighbor hobbled over on her cane. A few months back, Miss Mabel stopped by to drop off Valentine's Day cookies for me as a surprise. Aunt Shirley had answered the door with her nunchucks in hand and ended up swinging them around so much Aunt Shirley knocked herself out.

"Is everything okay?" Miss Mabel asked. "You aren't coming back here to stay, are you?"

The concern on Miss Mabel's face was genuine. Had anyone else in town asked me that question it would have been to snoop and see if Garrett and I had broken up.

"Everything's fine, Miss Mabel. Aunt Shirley, Old Man Jenkins, and I are just going to stay in town tonight here at the house. I want to turn on the heat so it will be warm when we come home tonight."

Miss Mabel frowned. "I heard on the police scanner something's happened at Lucy Stevenson's house."

I blinked in surprise. "Did they mention Lucy's house?"

Miss Mabel shook her head and smiled. "I've lived here my whole life. I know where everyone lives. I knew the minute they gave the address it was Lucy Stevenson's house." She leaned heavily on her cane, her body pitched forward. "It's not good, is it?"

I didn't know what to say. "No. Miss Mabel, it's not good."

Miss Mabel shook her head sadly. "What is this town coming to? So much crime and murder lately." She looked quickly at me. "Not that I'm blaming your nice young man. It's just so much different from when I was a little girl."

"I understand. And you're right, the town has changed a lot over the last few years."

Miss Mabel sighed. "I blame the city life. Those city people come to the small town and they bring with them their big city ways."

I bit my lip to keep from smiling. Wisely, I nodded my head but didn't contradict her. "You're probably right."

"Well, I have a wedding gift for you and your nice young man. I can't attend the reception. I'm just not up to it, you understand?"

"Of course. And you didn't have to get us a gift, Miss Mabel!"

Miss Mabel gave me a smile. "It isn't much. An Irish blessing, really. I hope you enjoy it. I'll bring it by later tonight."

"Sounds great."

She turned around and hobbled back over to her house.

The inside of my house was so cold, I was surprised penguins weren't waddling about and sliding on ice. I turned the heat up to a livable temperature, closed and locked the front door, then headed back to the Falcon.

CHAPTER 9

"I just can't believe this." Mom tied off a burgundy ribbon around a napkin full of plastic silverware. "Lucy Stevenson is dead."

Now that I'd told Mom and Paige what had happened to Lucy, I was having second thoughts about staying at my place in town tonight. I really didn't want to be away from Mom's side now that I was here.

"What do you suppose the note means?" Paige asked as she grabbed another set of silverware and wrapped it inside a napkin.

We'd spent the last hour cutting purple, burgundy, and orange ribbons and tying them around the napkins for our wedding guests. We were having our wedding meal catered from a Mexican restaurant in Brywood. Make-em-your-way tacos and nachos, along with Mexican rice and beans. Garrett and I were supplying the margaritas and beer.

"I honestly don't know," I said.

Mom scrunched her forehead. "Wasn't *Six Feet Under* a show? I think I remember back in like two thousand a show about a family that owned a funeral home. I never watched the show, but I think it was called *Six Feet Under*."

"That's just gross," Paige said.

"That does sound odd," Aunt Shirley agreed. "And I usually like odd. I'm surprised I never heard of it."

68

My phone vibrated. I glanced at the text then typed in my reply. "It's Hank. He said he and Mindy will be here around six. I told him not to eat dinner because Garrett was bringing subs."

"I don't mind making dinner," Mom protested. "It's really no trouble."

"We have enough to do without dirtying up the kitchen," I said.

Doc Powell and Old Man Jenkins walked into the room, each looking grave.

"We did as Hank suggested," Old Man Jenkins said. "We checked the perimeter of the house. No signs of footprints or broken twigs outside."

"Good deal," Paige said, rubbing her hands across her belly. "I don't know how much more of this I can take. I know all this stress isn't good for the twins."

"It's not," Mom said adamantly. "While you could deliver these babies safely any time now, I'd like to see you go another week."

"Don't worry," I joked, "when Mindy gets here she'll fill you full of herbal tea and you'll be so relaxed you may actually sleep through the night."

Paige laughed. "That would be an outright miracle!"

Doc Powell and Old Man Jenkins went back into the living room to keep watch...and watch TV. They weren't fooling anyone.

At precisely six o'clock, pounding followed by a gruff demand alerted us to the fact Hank and Mindy were here. Doc let them in while Mom went to put the kettle on the stove. First thing Mindy would want was a cup of hot herbal tea.

I leaned over and snatched a chocolate truffle off the counter and shoved it in my mouth.

Aunt Shirley slapped me on my hand. "I'd suggest not doing that again, chunkers. Unless you want us to shove you into *two* pairs of Spanx on your wedding day."

I scowled at her but continued chewing then swallowed the chocolatey gooey morsel. "You're right. I could use something else." I got up from the table and went to snatch a bottle of high-end bourbon out of Mom's cabinet. Pouring in two fingers worth of booze, I slowly tipped the glass up to my mouth and savored the flavors.

"Better?" Aunt Shirley asked as Paige snickered at me.

"Much."

I sat back down at the table and grabbed a set of silverware and a napkin.

"Jeez, Sinclair, are you ever gonna *not* get yourself in a mess?" Hank grumbled as he ambled into the kitchen, followed closely by Mindy. "I keep asking Kimble if he's sure he wants to go through with this whole wedding shindig and hitch himself to your accident-prone butt."

I scowled at Hank. "Just hush up or I won't have you officiate for us."

Hank barked out a laugh. "Ain't no one else gonna do it and you know it."

"Now, Hank, you leave her be," Mindy said as she made her way over to the stove. "These poor girls are stressed enough without you ribbing them."

I sent Mindy a grateful smile. "Thank you, Mindy."

"Jenkins around here?" Hank asked Aunt Shirley.

"I think he's in the living room pacing and muttering to himself about me getting wrapped up in danger around every turn or some such nonsense like that. I left him to his pacing and muttering."

Hank saluted us and marched out of the room toward Mom's living room.

"I can't believe this Danner guy has killed Lucy," Mindy said as she took down five mugs from the cabinet.

"I know," I moaned.

Mom sent me a sympathetic smile and got up from the table. She opened a cabinet and took down a bottle of cinnamon whiskey. She obviously knew I needed a little something-something in my tea.

"Will Garrett alert the town about this Danner character?" Mindy asked.

"I honestly don't know," I said. "We can't *prove* right now it's Danner. I guess he can alert people via social media that there's been a murder, but I don't think he can give specific details or descriptions. But I honestly don't know."

"I'll send Matt a text and see if he's going to post anything," Paige said. "He's usually in charge of keeping up with the social media page."

"On the bright side," Aunt Shirley said, "at least the killer isn't a citizen of Granville. And we don't have to figure out the killer. We know who it is, we just have to figure out where he's hiding out."

Mom delivered the doctored herbal tea cups to both Aunt Shirley and myself. I smiled in gratitude.

"Anything new on that?" Mindy asked.

I shrugged. "I think Garrett has checked the local hotel, and of course he's not there. No one matching his description is there. He's checked local campsites, too. Other than that, it's a toss up as to where Danner could be hiding out. Granville isn't that big, but big enough someone could blend in out in the country settings if they needed to."

"Wanna see my wedding rehearsal outfit?" Aunt Shirley asked.

I groaned. In all the chaos, I'd forgotten I was going to demand to see Aunt Shirley's outfit before she wore it to the rehearsal dinner. I'd hand-picked her bridesmaid dress, so I knew what that looked like, but I had no idea what she was wearing to the rehearsal dinner.

"Do I *want* to see it?" I asked tentatively.

"Yep." Aunt Shirley said. "I bought it special for this occasion. I figured since I'm in the wedding party, I better dress like I'm in the wedding party. You know what I mean?"

"No," I said. "I'm wearing a simple black dress."

Aunt Shirley waved her hand in the air. "A simple black dress? How does that scream BRIDE? Don't worry, I'll more than make up for your lack of haute couture. I'll just go get my suitcase out of the Falcon and put it on."

She bolted from the table and out the door. It was on the tip of my tongue to tell her to take someone with her for protection, but she was gone before I could even process where she was going.

"Wanna take bets on how bad it's going to be?" I asked grimly.

Mom grinned. "It's gonna be bad. The fact she used the word haute couture tells me all I need to know."

"I'm thinking 1860s *Gone with the Wind*," Paige said. "Hoop skirt and all."

"I'll take 1960s go-go dancer," Mindy giggled.

Mom shrugged. "Punk rock?"

I groaned. "Please no!"

A few minutes later Aunt Shirley lumbered back in, dragging her suitcase and makeup bag behind her. "I got lucky and found a dress on the Internet with your wedding colors in it. There's both deep purple and burgundy. Just give me a second. I'm gonna do a little makeup so you get the full effect. I took a picture of the model with my cell phone so I'd be able to copy it exactly."

I got up to get more hot tea...then thought better of it. Instead, I went over to the bottle of cinnamon whiskey and poured it straight in my mug.

Paige laughed. "Ryli Jo!"

"Don't judge me," I laughed. "I've earned this."

We made small talk for about fifteen minutes until Aunt Shirley finally finished.

"Are you ready?" Aunt Shirley called from down the hall.

"No. But I guess as ready as we'll ever be," I hollered back.

I lied.

I would never be ready for what came around that corner.

"Ta-dah!" Aunt Shirley cried as she flung her arms out, then turned in a wide circle.

The top half of the dress was a deep purple—almost black—crushed velour that hugged so tight it actually *lifted* Aunt Shirley's sagging boobs. The bottom was a princess poofy style that went all the way to the ground and was done in a burgundy satin with a black tulle overlay. When she twirled, she practically lifted herself off the ground. The only light color she had on was the white in her hair that wasn't already dyed either purple, burgundy, or orange. She'd tried to give herself a smokey eye—but it came out looking like she'd been beaten black and blue and purple. Her lipstick was a purplish black.

On a positive…no one won the bet.

Aunt Shirley had gone Goth.

Princess Goth to be exact.

CHAPTER 10

"I do have some good news." Garrett set the platter of subs down on the kitchen table. I was glad for the food. After Aunt Shirley's Goth debacle, I'd needed a lot more booze to keep from coming unglued. I was hoping the bread would help absorb some of the alcohol. "I got a call from someone out by Old Highway 6, wanting to report a suspicious person."

"And?" I asked.

"By the time I got there the person was gone, but there was definitely signs of someone having stayed there. Now, that's no guarantee it was Danner, but I'm trying to be positive."

"You're right," I agreed. "It's something."

Garrett leaned over and gave me a kiss on the cheek.

Meow!

I felt Miss Molly rub against my legs and leaned down to pick her up. "Thanks for bringing her here instead of dropping her off at the cottage here in town."

"I knew you'd want to see her."

I nuzzled my chin against her cheek and smiled as she purred loudly. "That, and I've been thinking about spending the night here with Mom and everyone else."

"There's plenty of room," Mom reassured me.

"It'll be like old times," Paige squealed. "You and I can sleep together in your old room."

"Old Man Jenkins and I can take Matt's room," Aunt Shirley said as she sipped on the margarita she'd made for herself.

Matt groaned.

"Doc and I can take my room." Mom's blush spread over her face, and she busied herself by getting out paper plates.

"And Hank and I can take the couch downstairs," Mindy offered, trying to ease Mom's discomfort.

"Yeah," Hank agreed. "I want to be downstairs so I can keep an eye on things."

"Then it's settled," Garrett said. "Guess you're staying here. Although I was going to have Officer Ryan keep an eye on both this house and your house, so I'm sure you would have been ok."

I frowned. "Maybe if we put a car in front of the cottage, Danner might think I'm home there and make a move."

Garrett smiled. "That's actually not a bad idea."

"You can take my DeVille," Old Man Jenkins offered.

Aunt Shirley cackled and took another drink of her margarita. "You remember the DeVille, don't ya, Ace? The car I used to run your skinny butt over."

I sighed and cut Garrett off before he could reply. "You didn't run him over. You ran his *car* over."

"Oh, much better," Garrett grumbled.

In her haste to come to my rescue last year, Aunt Shirley had coerced Old Man Jenkins into letting her drive his 1975 Cadillac Coupe DeVille. Aunt Shirley had plowed the car right into the side of Garrett's police-issued truck. And when he went to give her a ticket for reckless driving and driving without a license, she tore the tickets up in his face.

"Anyway," Old Man Jenkins continued, "you can use it and park it in her driveway so it looks like someone's home."

"Thanks." Garrett said. "I figure if Danner's been watching Aunt Shirley and Ryli, he knows where Ryli's old house in town is, and where Janine lives. So if we move a car over to Ryli's old house, I can keep Officer Ryan on patrol on Ryli's side of town. Matt and Hank will have this place covered—Matt from the outside and Hank from the inside, and I'll patrol the rest of the streets in down."

"Do you think you'll find him?" Mom asked.

Garrett nodded. "He'll mess up sometime, Janine. And when he does, I'll be there."

We ate dinner and went over plans and thoughts as to where Danner might be hiding. Mid-way through dinner Aunt Shirley got a call from her friend in Los Angeles regarding his search of Danner's house.

"My guy says Danner hasn't picked up his mail in days, and there're no lights on in the house. It's locked up nice and tight. He says it looks like Danner's fled. He said he'd be willing to call in favors to get the parole officer out there, but I told him not to. The parole officer was going to Danner's house tomorrow anyway. It's not like anything could be done before morning."

"Agreed," Garrett said. "Maybe if it were Wednesday, I'd say yes…but now we just play the hand we were dealt."

Aunt Shirley grinned. "Now you're talking my language."

After dinner Garrett drove Old Man Jenkins to the Manor so he could get his DeVille and park it at my cottage in town, then hitched a ride back with Garrett to Mom's house. I said goodnight to Garrett and he promised to keep me informed of what's going on.

After he left, I figured I'd be too wound to sleep, but by eight o'clock I was yawning and ready for bed. Paige and I said goodnight to everyone and slowly made our way upstairs.

"Your wedding rehearsal is tomorrow," Paige said as she turned down the bed covers. "Are you excited or can you even think about it right now?"

"Both? Is that a possible answer?"

"Yes. I just wish for once you weren't dealing with something crazy. This should be a stressful time because you're getting married, not because some maniac is trying to get to Aunt Shirley via you or someone else in the family."

I shrugged, knowing what she said was true. But I'd almost gotten used to the idea that no matter what I plan, something crazy is gonna come along and derail it.

"Um, what is that?" I asked when Paige threw a long, tubed pillow onto the bed.

"It's my body pillow. It's supposed to help me with positions when I'm trying to sleep. The twins are killing me."

I crawled under the covers and watched her struggle to get her otherwise-petite frame down on the bed and shimmy over to the pillow. Sweat broke out on her forehead.

"How does it help?" I asked.

Paige wrestled with the pillow and finally had it positioned behind her. She was panting heavily. She wrapped one leg around the bottom half of the pillow and pulled it close, causing the pillow to be wedged between her legs. She then tucked the top of the pillow under her head. She looked like she'd just ran a 5K marathon.

"You okay?"

Paige closed her eyes and nodded. "Yeah. It's a body pillow and it's supposed to help me sleep better at night. I'm okay once I get into position. I'm supposed to sleep on my left side according to the articles I've read."

"Why?"

"I don't know. Something about your liver being on your right side and doctors not wanting the babies to be pressed down on it." She reached up and wiped off the sweat at her brow. "I don't know if it's true or not. But I will tell you one thing that *is* true...I need these babies out of me. I'm so freaking miserable." Paige closed her eyes and tried to get her breathing under control.

I chewed on my lower lip. Just looking at her had me worried about my future. I wanted to be married to Garrett, I just wasn't sure I wanted what Paige was dealing with now.

"But it's all worth it, right?" I asked, hoping to hear gushing words of love and encouragement.

Paige opened one eye and the devil himself came out of her voice box. "I'm carrying around an extra forty-five pounds, I have four legs and four arms kicking every vital organ I have inside my body at all times of the day, my feet are the size of watermelons, I have the worst heartburn imaginable, my back spasms, my legs cramp, and I haven't pooped in—"

"Okay, okay! I get it! I'm sorry I asked. Honest!"

Paige closed her one eye again and took a deep breath in and then let it out. "I love them, though. And I can't wait to see them, whatever they are."

I was the only person who knew the sex of the babies. Paige, Matt, Mom…no one else knew. Just me. It was a big responsibility. Especially when I got excited talking about them. I had to remember to call them The Twins and nothing else.

"I can rub your back for you," I offered meekly.

Paige smiled at me. "You're the best friend I ever had, Ryli Jo. I'm so lucky to have married into your family."

I brushed a tear from my eye. "Why're you making us cry on the night before my wedding rehearsal? I don't want to have a swollen face tomorrow."

Paige gave a watery laugh. "Sorry." She swiped at her own tears. "But you are. And no, I don't need you to rub my back. What I need you to do is help Matt, Garrett, and Aunt Shirley capture this Danner fellow."

"Me? That's their job."

Paige laid her hand on my arm. "No, Ryli, whether you want to admit it or not, it's also your job. You're so smart. I know you can figure this out. From what Matt's told me, this guy has left a note behind at every scene. You can put those clues together. Garrett, Matt, and Aunt Shirley, they can brutally take down the guy…but you are different. You're like the brains while they are the brawn. You can put those clues together when the time comes and solve this case."

"Thanks for the vote of confidence." I knew it wasn't all true. The last murder that we were a part of, the corporate espionage, it was Aunt Shirley that put the clues together and figured out how the messages were being delivered.

"Good night, Ryli. Sleep well because the next two days are gonna be crazy."

If only they'd be crazy because of the wedding and not because a murderer was trying to kill us.

I had just drifted off when a pounding on my bedroom door startled me awake.

"Ryli? Paige?" Mom's voice came warbling through the door. "Are you girls awake?"

"We are now." I looked at the clock. Eight-fifty. "Come on in. What's going on?"

Mom opened the door, the light from the hallway illuminating her pale face. "Get dressed. There's been another murder."

CHAPTER 11

"Who?" I asked as I grabbed onto the doorframe of the kitchen. Mindy, Mom, and Aunt Shirley were already in the kitchen. I could hear the men talking in the front room.

Paige wedged her body next to mine in the doorway.

Mindy handed Paige and me a glass of hot herbal tea. I took it out of habit.

"Who?" I demanded again.

Mom met my eyes. "Your neighbor, Miss Mabel."

The cup slipped from my grasp and fell onto the floor with a loud crash. I looked down at the fallen cup. Luckily it hadn't shattered, just spilled.

"I'll get it," Mindy said quickly. "You go sit down at the table."

I bit my lower lip to keep from crying as I stumbled to the diminutive table Mom kept in the kitchen for quick meals. For more formal dinners we ate in the dining room.

"How?" I asked.

Mom and Aunt Shirley came over to the table and sat on each side of me.

"She must have seen Waylon's car in the drive and thought we were all home," Aunt Shirley said. "When we didn't answer, she probably went to go get the key you left her and let herself in your house. There was a wedding gift next to her body."

I looked at her in confusion. Then shook my head. "No. I mean how did she die?" My words came out in a sob.

Aunt Shirley looked at Mom before answering. "Quickly. You could tell Danner was enraged."

I could hear Paige crying softly behind me.

"That's one good thing," Mom said as she stroked my arm.

"Yes," Aunt Shirley agreed. "He was so angry he didn't think to torture her or prolong her death. He just ended her life quickly."

"Did he leave a note?" I asked. "He's been leaving notes."

Aunt Shirley and Mom exchanged looked.

"What?" I said. "Just tell me."

"He left *me* a note," Aunt Shirley said. "It basically said he was done playing games and someone I love will die within the next forty-eight hours. And then it will be my turn."

Paige let out a sob and covered her mouth with her hands.

"At least this should prove to Los Angeles that it's Danner," I said, trying to ignore my sorrow and rapid heartbeat.

"I don't think it matters anymore," Aunt Shirley said. "Garrett is done messing with California. We're on our own, and we will make sure Danner is captured before he can make good on his promise."

I laid my head down on my arms and wept for Miss Mabel. She was a sweet old lady that constantly watched out for me. When I lived in town, she would slip into my house and leave me cookies or some of her left-over dinner. Mabel was a kind and generous woman.

And now she was dead.

Rage flooded my body, and I wanted nothing more than to beat Danner within an inch of his life. How *dare* he think he had the right to come into *my* town on *my* wedding day and kill *my* friends. That psycho was going down and going down hard!

Miss Molly must have sensed my emotions because she jumped up onto my lap and started to knead my leg and purr. I gathered her close and nuzzled her neck.

Feeling better, I lifted my head off Miss Milly and stared at Aunt Shirley. "We're done playing defense. Now we move to offense."

Aunt Shirley's grin split her face. "That's my girl!"

"Who has their cell on them?" I asked.

"I do," Aunt Shirley said and handed me her cell.

Mindy looked questioningly at Mom...who shrugged.

I punched in Legends number and got the message machine. I didn't doubt I would. Usually Legends is closed by eight or whenever the last service is provided.

I decided to leave a message. "Daphne, this is Ryli Sinclair. Listen, I was wondering if you could please call me back as soon as you get this message. Doesn't matter the time. There's a lot of terrible things going on in Granville right now, and I think you may be able to help stop it."

I put my hand over the phone. "Does she have your number in case it doesn't pop up on her caller ID?" I asked Aunt Shirley.

"Yes."

I nodded and spoke back into the phone. "Daphne, you have Aunt Shirley's number, so just give us a call at whatever time you get this. My plan is to be at Legends tomorrow around eight. We need to get a jump start on this matter."

I hung up and punched in the police station's number.

"Granville Police Department," Claire Hickman said. "How can I help you?"

Claire Hickman had been the dispatcher at the police station for as long as I could remember. She was a plump, curly-haired woman who loved velour jogging suits and gossip. Working dispatch allowed her to participate in both her loves.

"Claire, it's Ryli. Don't say anything out loud about it being me. Are you working the midnight shift tonight?"

Claire paused. "It's okay, Ryli, Garrett and everyone is still over at Mabel's place. I just can't *believe* this is happening!"

"I know. Me, either. So, what's your schedule look like in the morning?"

"Lydia Marlin is coming in to relieve me around midnight tonight. Garrett told me to go home and get some rest. I come back on around nine tomorrow morning, why?"

"Because I plan on getting this SOB that's terrorizing our town," I said with more conviction than I actually felt.

"Good for you! Not that I don't think for one second that Garrett and the boys can't get this dastardly beast, but I'm glad you and Aunt Shirley are helping."

"Meet me at Legends around eight."

"Legends? Okay. You got it."

"And, Claire, bring along your best gossiper. I'm going to need the help of people who *really* knows what goes on in this town."

"Ooohhh, I don't know what this is about…but I like it! I'll be at Legends with Hattie at eight."

I hung up and handed the phone back to Aunt Shirley.

"So what's all this about?" Aunt Shirley demanded.

"It's time to let Danner in on the perks of living in a small town. He thinks he can hide from us, but he doesn't know the first thing about secrets and nosey women in this town."

Aunt Shirley gave me a high-five.

"Please be careful," Mom said. "I know I sound like a broken record, but I just worry about your safety."

"I'll be careful, I promise." I gave Mom a kiss on the cheek. "I got too much to lose right now to be completely foolish."

I heard the front door open and Garrett's voice ring out. I stood up and ran to him when he strode into the room. He held me close and whispered comforting words in my ear.

"I can't believe Danner killed Miss Mabel," I sniffed and looked up into his handsome yet tired face. "She was such a sweet, caring woman."

"I know." He brushed back my bangs and kissed my forehead. "I promise you, Ryli, we will get him."

I know you will...with a little help from Aunt Shirley and me.

Aunt Shirley's phone went off. She excused herself from the room and answered it.

"I have some hot coffee ready," Mom said to Garrett. "Would you like some?"

"That would be great, Janine. I really just came over to see how Ryli was holding up."

"I'll be okay," I said. "Just sad."

"I got something for you, Ace," Aunt Shirley whooped as she came into the kitchen. "I just got off the phone with my retired friend. He still has some pull over at homicide. So he asked around about new cases this week. There was a female that was killed three blocks from Danner's place Monday mid-morning. Right

86

now, the police are looking at the husband because two years ago there was a domestic dispute filed. But my friend thought we'd be interested because the husband keeps insisting it's not him and that the killer took off with his wife's car. Of course, the police think the husband did something with the car, but I'm thinking my friend might be on to something."

"Make and model?" Garrett said as he got out his notepad from his pocket.

"It's a 2012 Honda Civic. Dark grayish blue color."

"Thanks." Garrett stood up and grabbed the mug Mom had set down in front of him. "Janine, can I take this with me? Your coffee is a hundred times better than the station's coffee."

"You bet." Mom leaned over and kissed Garrett on the cheek. "Now you be careful out there tonight. We still have a wedding in two days to get ready for."

Garrett grinned at Mom. "I'm looking forward to it."

With one more farewell kiss, Garrett sauntered out the door and into the dark of night. A few minutes later and Doc, Old Man Jenkins, and Hank ambled into the kitchen.

"Well, we've done another perimeter check outside," Hank said. "Everything looks okay for right now."

"I'm exhausted," I said. "I think I'm ready to go back upstairs and sleep. There's nothing I can do for poor Miss Mabel right now."

Meow!

I knelt down and picked up Miss Molly. Tears filled my eyes as I rubbed her face against mine. "I'm so glad Garrett didn't drop you off tonight at the cottage like he originally planned."

Purr! Purr!

Once again, Miss Molly's vibration soothed my hurt just a fraction. I couldn't even stand to think about what I'd have done if Miss Molly had been in the house when Danner stopped by. He was obviously a cold-hearted evil man. He probably wouldn't have thought twice about hurting Miss Molly. It obviously didn't bother him to kill harmless old ladies.

"Paige," Mom said, "you two go on up to bed. You both look like you are about to keel over."

Paige gathered me and Miss Molly up in her arms and turned us toward the arched doorway. "C'mon. We both need some sleep."

"You're right," I said as I let her guide me from the room. "I need to make sure I'm nice and rested for when I confront Danner and rip him a new one!"

CHAPTER 12

"What on Earth are you wearing?" I asked as Aunt Shirley walked into the kitchen at seven-fifty the next morning.

Aunt Shirley preened and did a turn for Mom, Mindy, Paige, and me. "You like? I figured since we were going to be sleuthing today, I needed a good sleuthing outfit. So I put a couple of pieces together. Did a sort of miss-match thing."

I actually recognized some of the outfit. The pants were the black leather skin-tight pants that Aunt Shirley had ordered off a naughty website when we went to the murder mystery weekend a few months back. The good news...she wasn't wearing the matching leather button-up vest. Instead, she had on a black, long-sleeved turtleneck with the words STOP OR I'LL SHOOT in neon pink. Her white orthopedic tennis shoes stood out like a beacon in the night.

"Those pants can't be comfortable," I said. "In fact, I know they aren't. You said so the last time you wore them."

"But they look bitchin', right?" Aunt Shirley said as she strutted around the kitchen, pretending to draw a weapon.

"What if we have to run?" I said.

Mom moaned. "I'm not sure what's worse, thinking of Aunt Shirley running in those pants or the simple fact that you would have to run for your lives."

I held up a hand. "I'm not saying we *will* have to run, just what *if* we need to run. How are you gonna run in those?"

Aunt Shirley stopped in front of me. "Is it because you're jealous? Now that you've chunked up a little bit before the wedding and probably can't fit into leather pants, you have to belittle me?"

I shook my head in amazement. "First of all, I haven't *chunked up*. And I'd appreciate it if you'd stop saying that! And secondly, I'd never be caught dead in leather pants."

Aunt Shirley grinned. "Then you don't know what you're missing. Old Man Jenkins loves this outfit. The leather pants, the leather vest, the riding whip. Makes his day when I put this outfit on."

"Eww!"

"Stop!"

"Aunt Shirley!"

Paige, Mom, and Mindy covered their ears and squished up their faces. I was so immune to most of Aunt Shirley's ridiculous talk it hardly ever bothered me anymore.

"Fine. You can wear it." I said. "But if we have to run, I'm not carrying your butt. I'll leave you where you are."

"Ryli Jo!" Mom exclaimed. "You can't leave your aunt alone to get hurt!"

"Actually, I can. And I will. She knows the score. She wants to go all ridiculous, fine. But I won't be responsible for what happens."

Aunt Shirley grinned and did a few stretches and squats in her skin-tight leather pants. "The day you have to carry my butt around will be the day you need to put me out to pasture."

"Sweeter words I've never heard," I countered.

In truth, this was just casual banter between Aunt Shirley and me. It helped to get us ready for the upcoming event. I don't know how or why...but it just did. The more we ribbed each other, the more prepared we were for a mission.

"We're heading to Legends," I told Mom. "Once we leave there, I'll check in with you, okay?"

Mom bit her lip. I could tell she was struggling, but she held it in well. "Please do. And don't forget, Ryli, you're getting married tomorrow. Your wedding rehearsal starts tonight at five."

"We'll be back before then," I said. "If you need us to get anything while we're out, just call and let me know."

Mom, Paige, and Mindy gave us each a hug and kiss. They acted like we were going off to war instead of discovering Danner's hiding spot. The men were in the living room discussing strategies when Aunt Shirley and I walked in.

"You two be careful," Doc said. "I still gotta walk you down the aisle tomorrow, Ryli."

I smiled and kissed him on the cheek. "We'll be safe, I promise."

Aunt Shirley and Old Man Jenkins squabbled for a few more minutes before Aunt Shirley announced she was ready to go.

"Ryli," Hank said. "Are you guys armed?"

I looked at Aunt Shirley. "Aunt Shirley has her revolver."

"And my nunchucks and ninja stars," Aunt Shirley announced proudly, pounding on her pink oversized purse.

Hank smirked and shook his head. "Be careful. But not too careful. I expect a front-page story."

"And you'll get it!" Aunt Shirley declared.

"Right now we're just headed to Legends," I said. "I have an idea on how to find Danner. After that we'll call and give our whereabouts."

It only took a couple minutes to go from Mom's driveway to downtown Legends. I parked the Falcon in front of the store so we could keep an eye on it. I didn't want Danner messing with my pride and joy ever again.

Daphne and Claire were already inside the salon, as were the three other stylists at the salon Cindy Troyer, Brandy Thompson, and Tina Anderson. Standing by the coffee pot was Hattie Abernathy. Hattie was the reigning Queen of Gossip that went on in Granville.

"Good morning, ladies," Aunt Shirley said as we both walked farther into the room to join them.

"Not so good a morning," Hattie grumbled. "Mabel's dead."

I flinched. Knowing it was my fault. The poor woman had been in my house giving me a wedding gift when she was attacked.

"That makes two murders in as many days," Cindy said. "What're the cops doing about this?"

I held up my hand. "Let me start at the beginning."

I filled them in on who we believed the murderer to be and why. Then we talked about why he would go after both Lucy and Miss Mabel.

Daphne swirled her cup of coffee. "I did see on the Granville Police Department social media page this morning they were asking citizens to be on the lookout for someone hiding out in the country. They didn't give a name, just a suspicious person."

"I heard Garrett talking about it with Matt before I clocked out last night," Claire said. "I didn't know it had gotten posted."

I nodded. "But I think we can beat this Danner at his own game."

"How?" Brandy asked.

I looked over at Aunt Shirley before continuing. Just her presence could give me the courage I needed. "I don't think Danner is hiding out in Brywood or Kansas City. That's too far of a drive. He wants to keep us close."

"That's just horrible," Daphne said.

I nodded. "But true. The police have their way of doing things, protocols they follow, and I get that. But I think *we* can find Danner. Garrett and the guys are looking at obvious places…hotel, campgrounds. But Danner is also keeping the police department so busy with the stalking and threats and now the murders, that there aren't enough policemen to check every abandoned house and building in Granville and the outskirts. I think Danner knew what he planned on doing well in advance. He's been out on parole for a while now. Plenty of time to research Granville. This morning, I did a search on the Internet for country property in Granville. I got a couple of hits that stood out to me."

"What does that have to do with where Danner is staying?" Hattie asked. "And with us for that matter?"

I smiled. "Because you guys are on the inside. You girls knows all the ins and outs of this town. You are in on both the juicy gossip and where such rendezvous may take place."

Daphne pursed her lips. "You think Danner is lying low in an abandoned barn or something?"

"Something like that. I wrote down a bunch of places off the Internet that I believe he may be. I thought you guys could help me eliminate some of these places and even add some of your own.

Where might someone go if they wanted to be alone and not get caught somewhere?"

Brandy grinned. "Laura Estes got caught doing the nasty with Nicholas Tavoni out at the old Kealey place a couple months back. The house has been abandoned for about four years now."

"That place was on the Internet." I put a checkmark by the Kealey residence to check out.

Cindy nodded. "And don't forget last year when Mark Peckman's wife caught him hiding out at the old Cotton Mill during the day because he was afraid to tell her he'd lost his job in Kansas City."

"The Cotton Mill might be too obvious," Aunt Shirley said. "Garrett has probably thought about that place."

"Yeah," I said. "The Cotton Mill did come up on my search, but I agree it's too public."

Daphne took a drink of her coffee then set it on her counter. "I'm afraid I haven't been here long enough to really know places in Granville, and if they're popular or not. I do know that the kids like to hang out at this supposedly haunted house off C Highway."

"Garrett knows about that place," Claire said. "He goes out there quite a bit to bust up underage parties."

"What about the Sawyer place?" Tina asked, her face turning pink. "I know they are still trying to sell it, but with the amount of damage done to the house they aren't having much luck."

I looked over my notes. "I actually do have the Sawyer place on my list."

Aunt Shirley. "Isn't that the house that sustained storm damage and the family abandoned it and moved to Kansas City when they received the settlement?"

Tina's nodded. "Um, sometimes when Tom and I want a few minutes away from the kids, we go out there."

"Tina!" Brandy laughed. "You naughty girl!"

We all laughed at Tina's obvious discomfort.

"There's the rock quarry," Hattie said. "But that's really more for hiding a body, not hiding out."

I jerked my eyes in surprise to Hattie. That was the last thing I ever thought I'd hear her say.

Hattie gave me a shrug and grinned.

"There's the abandoned barn off Cellars Road," Cindy said chuckling. "But that will probably be too public. Although, Danner wouldn't know that." Cindy looked at the calendar on the wall. "And he'd be pretty safe staying in the barn for a few more weeks."

I scrunched my forehead. "Am I missing something?"

Cindy coughed and looked at Aunt Shirley then back at me. "You know, because that's where the swingers are meeting next month. At least that's what I've heard."

"We have a swingers group in Granville?" I asked, shocked I hadn't heard about it. "I should probably go out there with my camera and take pictures."

Cindy's mouth dropped. "Ryli! You can't go out there and take pictures of those people!"

I shrugged. "Why not? Do they do any competitions?"

Hattie let out a bark. "Do you have any idea what a swingers group is?"

I nodded. "Well, yeah. Like swing dancing. You swing your partner around to music."

The girls burst into laughter. Hattie laughed so hard she snorted. I got the feeling they were laughing at me but I couldn't understand why.

"Ya know," Aunt Shirley said, "I think this is one you ask Garrett about and not us." Aunt Shirley laughed even harder, bending over at the waist. "In fact, you might ask Garrett to take you out there. Tell him you want to watch the swingers. Maybe even join in if it looks like fun."

Once again the girls doubled over in laughter. I felt my face heat up. I hated being the butt end of a joke, but I honestly had no idea why they were laughing at me.

Aunt Shirley straightened and held up her hand. "Okay, back to serious stuff. We believe Danner is driving a newer, dark Honda Civic. It's a pretty common car. Have you guys seen one in town?"

They all shook their heads.

"Maybe he's getting his supplies and food in Brywood," Hattie suggested.

I nodded. "Probably. But he's staying in Granville. I feel it. He has too many snapshots of Aunt Shirley and me running around town not to be close."

Brandy shivered. "That's just so scary to think about. You ladies be careful."

"We will," Aunt Shirley said pointing to me. "I gotta get this one married off this weekend."

Tina squealed. "That's right! I totally forgot with all this murder talk. Are you ready?"

I spent a couple more minutes doing the small talk routine with the gossips, knowing they'd want to have something to talk about with their clients today. Aunt Shirley told them about her dress for tonight, and they all oohed and aahed, but again I could see the humor in their eyes at the thought of her going Goth.

We left Legends a few minutes later and hopped in the Falcon.

"I'm feeling pretty good about the Kealey place, the Sawyer place, and the abandoned barn off Cellars Road you all laughed at me for. How about you?"

Aunt Shirley nodded. "Agreed. Let's go find us a killer."

I gave a small laugh. "First, we call Garrett and tell him what we found out and *then* we go with him to find us a killer."

Aunt Shirley scowled at me. "You know he ain't gonna let us tag along and help find Danner. He'll give us some BS about how it's a man's job."

I grinned mischievously at her. "But we got an in. We're consultants with the police department now, remember? Well, at least you are. We can worm our way in that way."

CHAPTER 13

"No. Absolutely not." Garrett paced back and forth inside his office before coming to a stop in front of me. He put one hand to the side of my face. "Ryli, I'm so proud of you for narrowing down our best places to look. I really am. That was brilliant thinking. But I can't risk you going out there with us. It would be reckless for me to agree to such a thing."

Aunt Shirley humphed. "So you're saying you don't mind us using our brains to help you out, but that's all we're good for?"

Garrett narrowed his eyes at Aunt Shirley. "Don't go putting words in my mouth."

Aunt Shirley nonchalantly lifted one shoulder. "I got me a PI license now. Nothing stopping me from investigating this matter. It was Ryli here who thought we should bring you in on *our* discovery."

Garrett's nostrils flared. I could tell by the tic in his cheek he was barely holding it together. I rested my hand on his arm. "Garrett, we deserve to go. Maybe I was off on my thinking…but I don't think so. And we're personally involved in this mess. I mean, he's gunning for Aunt Shirley."

Garrett closed his eyes and sighed. "Fine. You can come. I'll admit, I'd like to see you in action a little. I spend so much of my time trying to keep you from jumping into the fire instead of letting you get your feet warmed." His eyes flicked over to Aunt Shirley. "Make sure Aunt Shirley is teaching you the ropes correctly."

I heard Aunt Shirley growl and hid my smile. If Garrett was up to taunting Aunt Shirley, he couldn't be too upset with us.

"Let's hit Cellar's Road first, then the Sawyer house, and then the Kealey residence," I suggested.

Garrett gave me a strange look. "You realize the barn on Cellar Road isn't a viable hideout, right?"

"*You* know there's a swinging club out there, too?" I said.

Garrett's brows furrowed. "Yeah. I'm aware. They move locations all the time, and by the time I get wind of it, they change locations again."

Aunt Shirley cackled. "Ryli here thought maybe you and her should go out there one night, give it a try. She'd even take her camera along to film it."

Garrett's mouth dropped open. "*What?*"

I threw up my hands. "Why is everyone having that reaction? I think it's cool the way they swing their partners around and around and flip them in the air. I guess it can be a little dangerous, but it's still pretty neat."

Garrett's mouth dropped open, then he gathered me close to his body and kissed the top of my head. "I love your innocence. Don't ever change."

"Where's Matt?" Aunt Shirley asked. "Is he riding out there, too?"

Garrett shook his head. "I have him and Officer Ryan manning phones from concerned Granville citizens and working on both murders. The parole office isn't open out in California yet, but I left another message that we've had another murder and what the note left at the scene said. We pretty much have Danner dead-to-rights now. I've demanded a phone call back once they confirm

Danner is no longer at his house in California. So I really can't afford to pull them from their assignments."

Aunt Shirley snickered. "So it's good for you our services are available."

Garrett snorted. "Must be my lucky day."

***

"Watch your rear-view mirror at all times and look for signs of being followed," Aunt Shirley said. "I don't want Danner to sneak up on us."

I had Aunt Shirley text Mom and tell her we were with Garrett and we'd be home within the hour. I knew if I called Mom and spoke with her, she'd just reiterate to me how worried she'd be for me. I was beginning to think that Garrett was dealing better with me getting my PI license than Mom.

I checked my rear-view mirror and pointed the Falcon out of town, trailing a safe distance behind Garrett's police-issued vehicle. I made a left on P Hwy and followed the curved road for five miles. Making a left on Culvers Road, I crept along at a slow pace over the gravel road.

I checked my rear-view mirror again. I didn't see any sign of a car on the road. "I'm looking for dirt flying up off the gravel road."

Aunt Shirley nodded. "That's the smart thing to do."

I saw the barn sitting back off the right-hand side of the road. I slowed down and turned right at the narrow, weed-infested path. I drove the fifty yards up to the dilapidated barn and stopped next to Garrett's vehicle. I manually rolled down the Falcon's window.

"Stay put until I clear the scene," Garrett hollered before taking out his gun and walking toward the barn.

My pulse raced at the thought of him going in there alone. "What if Danner's in there? Shouldn't you go with him?"

Aunt Shirley shook her head. "No. Ace knows what he's doing. But I think I will get out and look around the vehicles." She pulled her gun out of her purse and opened the door. I bent down and watched her survey the area.

"I don't see any recent tracks from a vehicle," Aunt Shirley said.

I scrambled around in Aunt Shirley's purse and took out her nunchucks and four ninja stars. I had no idea what good they would do me, but at least I'd have some protection.

"I'm not going to tell you again," Aunt Shirley said. "You need to start carrying around your gun."

I blew out an exasperated breath. "I *know*, Aunt Shirley. I just need to get my head there."

"Well, make sure you hurry and get your head there soon…before you go and get said head blown off."

I curled my lip at her but said nothing. Mainly because I knew she was right.

"It's clear!" Garrett yelled from the open barn door. "The stuff inside here is not from Danner but from the monthly parties."

I followed Aunt Shirley toward the barn, turning to stare over my shoulder and at the road to make sure a car wasn't coming. We would be easy targets for Danner out here.

I followed her into the barn, expecting the worst. I was mildly surprised to smell the lingering scent of vanilla and musk incense. There were numerous foam mattresses strewn about on the rotting, wooden floor and a plethora of blankets and pillows.

"I'd say there are tons of people camping out here," I said.

Aunt Shirley snickered. "Yeah. Definitely tons of people camping out here."

Garrett holstered his gun. "I don't think Danner would set up tent out here."

Aunt Shirley instantly sobered. "No. He wouldn't. Let's go see what we find out at the Sawyer place."

I turned and followed her back toward the entrance of the barn.

"Is that a pair of underwear?" I said, pointing to a wad by a moldy hay bale.

Aunt Shirley and Garrett both just snickered and walked out the barn door. Giving the abandoned underwear one more disdainful look, I scurried out the barn and ran back to the Falcon.

"That was a bust," Aunt Shirley said. "But I honestly expected it to be."

"Let's hit the Sawyer home next," Garrett said.

I was about to walk to the Falcon when Garrett pulled me into his arms. I giggled when he nuzzled my neck, but stopped cold when he whispered in my ear.

"Shut up!" I said. "No way!"

Garrett chuckled and kissed my forehead. "Way. That's what swingers really means."

My face flushed and I looked back toward the barn. Now the snickers at my suggestion to bring Garrett out here and film what was going on made more sense.

Wrapping his arms around me, we walked back to our vehicles.

"I take it he finally told you what swinging means?" Aunt Shirley said.

"I don't want to talk about it," I said primly. "I'll probably never be the same."

Aunt Shirley hooted and slapped her knee.

The Sawyer place was about ten miles from where we were. I hoped we'd have better luck over there.

"How're your vows coming?" Aunt Shirley asked.

I rolled my eyes. "Let's not talk about that right now. I haven't had time to even think about wedding stuff." I laughed sardonically. "Here I thought by now I'd be a nervous wreck, worrying about the wedding. But I haven't had time to even dwell on it."

Aunt Shirley flicked her top row of false teeth in and out of her mouth in a quick succession. "Glad my impending murder can be of help to ya."

I cringed as spittle went flying out of her mouth. I don't know why she'd suddenly developed that disgustingly annoying habit. "When are you gonna get your false teeth fixed? One of these days those teeth are gonna fall out at the worst possible time. And stop saying that. You aren't going to be murdered."

Aunt Shirley shrugged. "Fine. We'll talk about something else. So, how're your wedding vows coming along?"

Her shrill laugh rankled me, and I gripped the wheel so hard my knuckles turned white. Knowing I just needed to ignore her, I focused on following Garrett.

"I could help you write them like I did Paige's vows."

I shuddered. "No, thanks."

Garrett turned into the Sawyer place and I cut off the Falcon's engine beside him. The house looked appalling. The right half of the roof had been blown off, three front windows were missing, and the front porch was sagging so much I was afraid to go anywhere near it.

I rolled down my window and waited for direction.

"Same procedure," Garrett said. "I'll do a quick sweep."

"Can you get up on that porch safely?" I asked.

"Yeah. Aunt Shirley, would you mind covering the back for me?"

Aunt Shirley blinked in surprise. "Of course." She pulled out her gun and got out of the Falcon.

Garrett slowly made his way to the front of the house as Aunt Shirley cut around the back. I stuck my thumbnail in my mouth and started to gnaw. Then quickly stopped when I realized I might be ruining my wedding manicure.

A few minutes later Aunt Shirley came sprinting out from the backyard like her tail was on fire. "Skunk!"

I looked behind her and saw a black and white animal, tail high in the air. Trotting behind the skunk were three more tiny skunks.

"Calm down," Garrett hollered as he made his way out of the front of the house. "Skunks rarely spray unless provoked."

Aunt Shirley didn't slow down until she reached the passenger side door of the Falcon. Bending over, panting, she tried prying her leather pants off her legs. "These dang things are beginning to chafe."

"I told you not to wear them," I said dryly, my eyes never leaving the fast-approaching animals.

"It's okay," Garrett said again as he holstered his weapon and carefully crept through the front yard over to where we were.

"Okay?" Aunt Shirley repeated. "It's not okay." She pointed to the mother skunk. "That little demon is hissing at us!"

Garrett chuckled. "That's just a defense mechanism. The mother is showing her dominance because you disturbed her babies."

"Those ain't babies," Aunt Shirley grumbled, giving the animals the evil eye. "Those are demonic mini-mes waiting to attack."

I looked at Garrett. "I hope I'm right on this thinking. I really thought Danner would plan ahead and scope out the area before making his move."

Garrett nodded and crossed over to his police-issued vehicle. "I'm sure you're right. We still have the Kealey place left to sweep, so don't get too discouraged."

I sighed and got back into the Falcon, my heart heavy at the thought that I might have failed Garrett and Aunt Shirley. I'd been so sure about my theory. We pulled out of the driveway, leaving the skunks to go back inside their new residence, and made our way to the Kealey place.

"I just got a text from your mom," Aunt Shirley said as she looked up from her cell phone. "She needs us to stop off at Quilter's Paradise when we're done and pick up a couple more yards of burlap."

I was about to answer when I heard flicking sounds. I turned my head slowly to look at her. "Stop doing that with your false teeth…it's *disgusting*!"

"I can't help it. They're so loose now they just sorta fall out all the time."

"Well get them fixed! It's not like you can't afford it, right?"

Aunt Shirley shrugged. "No sense buying new when the old works just fine."

I rolled my eyes and did my best to ignore her and her false teeth.

CHAPTER 14

Within ten minutes Garrett pulled up to the Kealey house. It was an old, two-story farmhouse with dilapidated siding and damaged shingles. The front yard looked like it hadn't been mowed all year. Luckily the weight of the leaves falling from the numerous trees in the yard helped to flatten some of the grass.

"This place has gone to pot," Aunt Shirley sniffed.

I had to agree. I couldn't imagine the inside faired any better than the old Sawyer place as far as nasty creatures, either. Garrett bypassed the side drive and parked in the front yard. I parked next to Garrett and slowly got out of the Falcon as Garrett walked over to us.

"I don't want to be where I can't see what's going on," he said. "Parking in the side drive would leave me visually impaired."

"Good thinking," Aunt Shirley said.

"Aunt Shirley, do you want to take the front and I'll take the back this time?" Garrett chuckled. "Maybe the front won't be so overwhelmed with critters."

"Sure thing." Aunt Shirley pulled out her gun and with a wink to me headed toward the front porch.

"Hey," Garrett said, wrapping one arm around me but still watching Aunt Shirley. "I just want you to know that I think your theory is right on. It may not be one of these houses, and it may be we go back to the drawing board, but I think you're on to something here. I'm very proud of you."

"Thank you. That means a lot."

He was about to say something more when Aunt Shirley let out a curse.

"What's wrong?" Garrett said, immediately on alert.

"Nothing," Aunt Shirley said as she stopped in front of the door. "Just these dang teeth. Can't keep them in."

I looked at Garrett and rolled my eyes.

Boom!

I jumped three feet in the air and screamed.

"Dammit!" Garrett cried as he took off for the front door.

My brain took a few seconds to register the huge hole in the door and Aunt Shirley on the ground.

I started screaming again and took off after Garrett to where Aunt Shirley was lying on the ground.

"Aunt Shirley!" I screamed, trying to focus my brain enough to scramble up the three steps. "Omigod! Can you hear me? Are you dead?"

"No, I ain't dead. But I think I peed my pants."

"She's okay, Ryli," Garrett said gently. "She's fallen forward. If she'd been shot she'd have flown backward more. See, she's okay."

I swiped at the tears falling from my eyes, praying for my mind to focus on what Garrett was saying. But all I could hear was the gun blast, and all I could see was Aunt Shirley on the ground.

"I'm okay." Aunt Shirley grabbed hold of Garrett's outstretched hand and he pulled her to her feet.

"What happened?" I demanded.

"When I got to within two feet from the door, my dang teeth fell out. I bent to pick them up and while I was still down by the ground I just reached up and opened the door. I didn't have time to register how strange it was to be unlocked before the gun went off and I fell forward because I lost my balance from the sound and shock of it."

Garrett peeked through the hole. "Looks like he rigged up a pulley system."

"Shot gun?" Aunt Shirley asked.

"Yep," Garrett agreed.

I flung myself at Aunt Shirley. "My gosh, you could have *died!*"

Aunt Shirley patted my back then pushed me away from her. "But I didn't." She cut her gaze to Garrett. "Let's not make a big deal out of this."

Garrett said nothing for a few seconds. "I want you to go back to the Falcon. I'm going to check around in here. I don't expect to find anything, but just in case, I want to do a quick sweep. We'll talk in a minute."

Aunt Shirley nodded once then grabbed my arm and hauled me down the steps.

"Why're you dragging me?" I asked. "I can walk on my own."

"Keep quiet until we get to the car," Aunt Shirley hissed.

Offended, I yanked my arm out of her grip and stomped to the Falcon's driver's side door. Giving her one more death glare, I yanked open the door and plopped down onto the seat.

"Cool your jets," Aunt Shirley said. "I need you to pull yourself together and not make a big deal out of what just happened."

"Um…it *is* a big deal!"

"No, Ryli, it isn't." Aunt Shirley turned to me. "You understand that Garrett is right on the edge of embracing you working with him and getting your PI license. Investigation is something he's had reservations about for a year now. Right now, he's inside that house worried about how he's going to compartmentalize your safety with giving you the freedom you want. You go and make a big deal out of this, and he'll run scared. He'll go back to worrying that you and I don't have what it takes to do this job! So suck it up, buttercup. Put on your big-girl panties and go with my lead."

For a half second I wanted to tell her to bite me. To take her stupid logic and cram it. But just as quickly I realized she was right. I couldn't go running scared every time something bad happened and then expect to be taken seriously. Garrett was a by-the-book kind of guy. He needed to think I was safe at all times and that I could handle tense situations.

I balled my hands into fists so they'd stop shaking and took a deep breath. "You're right. I need to remember that Garrett needs to see me strong. See me as capable of handling myself in a difficult situation."

"Good girl."

A few seconds later, Garrett came marching out the front door and over to the Falcon. Aunt Shirley and I got out of the car and met up with him.

"It's clear," he said. "There're signs of someone staying there. I have no idea if he set that up his first night just in case someone entered and has been leaving the back way, or if he's staying someplace else because he thinks we're on to him. Either way, he's not here right now."

"At least Ryli's theory was right," Aunt Shirley said. "Very smart thinking, Ryli."

Garrett looked at me then at Aunt Shirley. "I know what you're doing here."

Aunt Shirley sighed. "Garrett Kimble, you just stop it right there. I know what you're gonna say, but you need to understand that we are just fine."

Garrett shook his head. "I just don't know about this."

"Why is it okay for you and not us?" I asked quietly.

Garrett let out a hallow laugh. "Because, God help me, I love the two of you. As exasperating as you both may be at times. I don't want to see either of you hurt."

"But why is it okay for you and not for us?" I asked again.

"Ryli, I've had extensive training. Both from my military days and my training from the police academy. I can protect myself and others. That's what I'm good at."

I laid my hand on his arm. "Yes, you are. But so are we. Maybe not like you, but we do have certain skills. I usually have good ideas and Aunt Shirley usually comes through at the end. It somehow works for us. We may not be as smooth and polished as you, Garrett, but we're a pretty good team."

Garrett clenched his jaw and looked out to the road behind me. He said nothing for a full twenty seconds. "You're right. It's been foolish of me to try and talk you out of this. If this is what you want to do, I'll stand behind you. And from here on out, instead of fight you, I'm going to see to it that you have proper training. You will learn to shoot, learn to track, and everything else Aunt Shirley and I need to do to protect your and keep you as safe as possible."

My heart leaped. "You mean it? You'll help train me for a future as a PI? Maybe even hire me and Aunt Shirley as consultants when you need extra help?"

Garrett ran his fingers through my hair and pulled me close. "I mean it. We'll consider it my first official wedding gift. I'll teach you everything I know."

Aunt Shirley let out a whoop as Garrett brushed his lips across mine.

CHAPTER 15

"How many yards of burlap did she need?" I asked Aunt Shirley as I carried the fabric to the cutting table.

"She said a couple, so I'd say five should do it."

I dropped the bolt onto the counter so Ronni Reynolds could start to measure and cut.

"How's everything going, Ronni?" I asked once she'd unraveled the five yards.

Ronni gave me a shy smile. "Pretty good. My side business is really picking up. I can hardly keep up with all the orders."

A few months back when Aunt Shirley and I were investigating the espionage and murder at Quilter's Paradise, Ronni was one of our top suspects because it seemed she suddenly came into a lot of money. When confronted, she admitted her secret was she was selling craft projects online from leftover scraps that Blair said she could have.

"That's great!" I said. "I'm glad to hear that."

"And I hear congratulations are in order for *both* of you," Ronni said as she gave Aunt Shirley a sly grin and started to make out a ticket. "Married in Vegas! Nicely done."

Aunt Shirley scowled. "It was stupid. It was one of those young and dumb things."

I snorted. "You, Aunt Shirley, are not young."

"Watch your mouth!" Aunt Shirley snapped. "Age is only a number. I'm way too young to settle down and be married."

Ronni winked at me as she handed me the fabric and ticket. "Well, I still think it's nice the two of you getting married so close together. Are you planning a co-honeymoon?"

"Why does everyone keep asking us that?" I asked Aunt Shirley.

Aunt Shirley shrugged. "Because it's a smart thing to do."

I let out a sharp laugh. "No, it's not!"

"Well, regardless, you have a good rest of the day," Ronni said. "I plan on stopping by for a little while at your reception, Ryli. I can't wait to see everything."

We thanked her and headed to the checkout register. I was beginning to feel guilty for leaving Mom so long. She had Mindy and Paige to help, but with Paige about ready to pop, I didn't imagine she was too much help.

"Well, well, if it isn't the soon-to-be blushing bride." Willa Trindle's syrupy fake voice was like nails on a chalkboard. "I'd have thought you'd be home primping for your rehearsal tonight."

I gave her a tight smile. "Last minute items to get."

She looked down at the burlap in my hand before yanking it out of my grasp. "Burlap? Are you doing a burlap and lace reception?" Willa looked down her nose at me. "How *quaint.*"

I bared my teeth at her. And I may have even growled. I'm not sure.

"The burlap is just in case we need to bury a dead body," Aunt Shirley said, her hard eyes never leaving Willa.

Willa understood the threat and her mouth dropped.

"You and your mom still planning on attending the social event of the season?" Aunt Shirley asked.

I hid a smile at her obvious taunt on my wedding being the social event of the season. I wouldn't exactly say it was the social event of the *season,* but it was a pretty big deal.

"Well, *I* am bringing Tristan Rainer, of course, because we're still dating." Willa leaned in conspiratorially. "You're *sure* you're okay with me bringing the boy you've had a crush on your entire life—and was never once reciprocated—to your wedding?"

I laughed at her pathetic attempt. "Willa, I'm getting married to the man I love. I don't give a rat's butt who you bring to the wedding *reception.*"

My shallow way of reminding her she wasn't invited to the wedding, just the reception.

Willa scowled. "Of course, the reception. And Mom is still bringing her new man. Wait until you meet him. He's a handsome one."

Aunt Shirley rolled her eyes at me. "Yes, I'm sure he is."

"How did they meet?" I asked.

Willa averted her gaze and shrugged. "On the internet, I think. I don't really remember."

Well, that's odd.

"How long have they been seeing each other?" Aunt Shirley asked.

"Not long. But he's handsome and charming, and Mom's crazy about him and he's crazy about her!"

Then there is definitely something wrong with him.

Willa handed me the bag. "See you tomorrow evening."

"Yep," Aunt Shirley said proudly, "when Ryli becomes Mrs. Ryli Kimble."

Tomorrow evening. Tomorrow night I would be Ryli Kimble. Mrs. Ryli Kimble.

"It's his funeral," Willa muttered.

My head jerked up at her whispered words. What had she meant by that?

"You okay?" Aunt Shirley asked as I got behind the wheel of the Falcon and rested my head on the steering wheel.

"No. I think I'm going to be sick. Do you realize tomorrow night I will be Mrs. Ryli Kimble? Am I ready for this?"

Aunt Shirley laughed. "As ready as you'll ever be." She brushed her hand across my shoulder. "You're gonna be fine, Ryli. There've been a lot of changes the last couple months, what with Paige and Matt having twins, me and Old Man Jenkins getting married, and now you and Garrett getting hitched. And the truth is, this is just the start. The next few months after this will be just as crazy. The twins will be here by then, I'll still be married to that crazy old man, and you and Garrett will be starting your life together, which will involve a whole new career. And who knows where your mom and Doc will be. I look for them to tie the knot soon, too."

"Wow!" I lifted my head up off the steering wheel. "One year ago I felt like my life was in a rut, nothing ever happened in this town, my job was going nowhere, I was going to be alone forever, and then in a blink of an eye, everything has changed."

"For the better, dear."

I gave her a weak smile. "I know. I'm just scared."

"Let's go home and fill everyone in on what has happened."

"You going to tell them *everything*?"

"Heck, yeah. That was Ace's crisis moment. The time when he stopped worrying about trying to protect you and realized he needed to teach you how to protect yourself. So, yeah, we're telling them everything."

I grinned at the thought of the lecture Aunt Shirley was going to get from Mom and Old Man Jenkins. Better her than me!

CHAPTER 16

"Are you *crazy?*" Mom shrieked when Aunt Shirley got to the part about nearly getting her head blown off.

Aunt Shirley shrugged. "Jury's still out on that."

"No, it's not." Old Man Jenkins folded his arms across his chest and gave Aunt Shirley the death stare.

I took another sip of my chardonnay and smiled into my glass. I tuned out the lecture Aunt Shirley was getting and focused on what I still had left to do before the wedding rehearsal. If my math was right, I had just over two hours before Garrett's mom and dad were due to arrive from Dallas. They decided to drive up so they could visit family and friends on the way home.

Since the actual wedding was going to be small and intimate, with Hank officiating and Old Man Jenkins and Doc walking me down the aisle, Paige as my Maid of Honor and Aunt Shirley my bridesmaid, Matt as the Best Man and Officer Mike Ryan as the groomsman, and Mindy taking photos, there really wasn't a need to have a set time for the rehearsal and dinner. But Mom wanted to keep with tradition. So we would be running through the ceremony and then have a light meal of cheeses, breads, finger hors d'oeuvres, and different wines.

"What time are the flowers and cupcakes being delivered?" I asked, hoping to steer the conversation away from the lecture Aunt Shirley was getting.

Miss Molly chose that moment to saunter into the kitchen and jump up on my lap. Out of habit I began petting her long hair.

"The flower shop said three o'clock for them, and Barbara called today and said she'd bring the cake, cupcakes, and cookies around four," Mom said. "Everything will be done beforehand except the flowers, so there's no reason a five o'clock wedding can't happen."

"Sounds good," I said. "What exactly did you need more burlap for?"

Mom's face turned pink. "You'll think I'm just being silly, but I'm going to line the trays with the burlap, and then put the lace on top of the burlap. This way the trays pop more."

I shook my head and smiled. Mom was such a stickler for the details. "Sounds great. You know if it was up to me I'd just slap some cookies on a tray and call it good."

Mom sighed. "I know."

"I got a text from Garrett a few minutes ago," Hank said. "He said the county sheriff is on his way out to the old Kealey house to look for evidence."

"Good," I said. "Then everything's on track and I can go take a bath and get ready for tonight."

Miss Molly jumped down off my lap as I stood. She turned and gave me a glare, letting me know she wasn't happy about being disturbed.

"I'll go up with you," Paige said. "I could use some rest."

I peered closer at her. "You look a little pale. Are you okay?"

Paige waved her hand at me. "Yes. I'm just a little tired. Lots of movement from the twins today." She rubbed her hand under her belly and sighed. "I know I sound like a broken record, but they need to come out soon."

"C'mon." I wrapped my arm around her shoulder and picked up my wine glass in the other hand. "We'll go upstairs and relax for a while. You can watch me drink wine and be jealous."

"Don't go getting too snockered," Hank hollered. "I'm already two days behind on next week's layout. I need your help getting caught up."

"Sure thing, boss," I said smartly. "Just give me an hour and I'll be down."

"Will you really?" Paige whispered to me.

I chuckled. "No. But he doesn't need to know that."

"I heard that, Sinclair," Hank shouted at my back.

"Hank, you leave that girl alone," Mindy said. "It's the night before her wedding. I know for a fact you've already prepared next week's layout."

I smiled at the chewing Hank was getting from Mindy. No one else would have the guts to stand up to the old curmudgeon that way. Mindy was my hero for a reason.

***

"Garrett's parents are in town," Mom said as Paige and I entered the kitchen an hour and a half later, dressed in my new black dress and ready for the wedding rehearsal.

I jerked back, started at that declaration. "How did you find out? He didn't text me."

Matt walked into the kitchen from the living room, devouring a plate of food.

"That's for after the rehearsal," I said dryly.

Matt shrugged and grinned as he popped another cube of cheese in his mouth. "I'm hungry, sue me." He swallowed the mouthful of cheese. "Anyway, Mom knows because I told her. Their first stop in town was to the police station to greet Garrett."

Garrett's parents…Howard and Bernadette Kimble.

I hadn't officially met them yet because they didn't get up to Missouri all that often. The last time they visited, Garrett and I weren't dating. He'd just started working for the Granville PD, so I had no reason to meet them. Now my first introduction will be as their future daughter-in-law. No pressure there.

"Where are his parents staying?" Mindy asked.

"They're staying at Garrett's house," I said. "It was supposed to be the four of us, but now that I'm staying in town, it will just be the three of them out there."

"Do you think that's safe?" Mom asked.

I nodded. "Garrett assured me both his parents are good shots. It's where he learned to shoot as a boy. They don't know what's going on, but when they find out, the three of them will have no problem defending themselves."

"Garrett said when he finished up at the office he'd bring them over," Matt said.

I wiped my hands on my dress. "Do I look okay?" I swiped another glass of chardonnay off the table.

"You look beautiful, dear." Mom leaned over and kissed my cheek. "I can't believe you're getting married tomorrow. My baby's getting married."

"How come you didn't get all weepy like this with me?" Matt grinned and winked at Mom.

"Oh, stop it. I got this weepy with you."

Paige wrapped her arms around Matt. "Stop teasing your mom. She's stressed enough."

"How are my future professional baseball players doing today?" Matt asked as he set his plate down on the table and wrapped his two hands around Paige's protruding belly.

"Your daughters are fine," Paige teased back.

Matt bent down and kissed Paige's stomach. "That's what I like to hear."

"Garrett's coming up the drive with his parents in tow," Old Man Jenkins hollered from the front room.

My stomach pitched and I grabbed onto the back of one of the kitchen chairs.

"Take a drink and breathe," Mom said. "Has anyone seen Aunt Shirley?"

"Oh, God," I moaned. "I forgot all about her and that crazy dress of hers."

"I think she's still upstairs getting ready," Mindy offered.

"I'll go get her," Old Man Jenkins said as he walked into the kitchen. "Otherwise she'll be up there all night."

"Is there anything I can do?" Doc asked.

"I think we're all set," Mom said. "We were really just waiting on Garrett and his parents."

A few minutes later Garrett and his parents walked into the kitchen. Introductions and hugs were being conducted when a cough came from the doorway.

"I hope I didn't miss everything," Aunt Shirley said.

"Oh my!" Bernadette Kimble said as she took in Aunt Shirley's outfit. "That's quite a dress."

Aunt Shirley preened and did a full circle, causing the tulle on her Goth skirt to billow out. "Thank you. I bought it special just for tonight."

I could tell by the look Bernadette gave Garrett, that he'd already warned her about Aunt Shirley.

"And I come bearing gifts for the bride and her maid-of-honor," Aunt Shirley said as she thrust a bag at Paige and me.

Terrified, I reached inside and moved the tissue around until I found the gift. I gingerly lifted it out of the bag. It wasn't exactly ugly…but it also wasn't my style. It was a huge, copper bracelet with a large knob on the top. "Thanks, Aunt Shirley."

Aunt Shirley snorted. "Do you know what that is?"

I looked at Paige…who shrugged.

"A bracelet?" I asked.

"Not just any bracelet. It's a booze bracelet! I ordered it off the Internet. See." She thrust her arm up to show me hers. She unscrewed the lid and lifted the bracelet up to her mouth and took a huge swallow. "Small and compact. Goes where you go. No more lugging around that huge booze purse I have. Now we can wear our booze in style! I had them inscribed with the words 'Bride Tribe' inside the band. Of course, I had to put water in Paige's, but yours, Ryli, has cinnamon whiskey in it."

Howard Kimble chuckled. "That's actually pretty ingenious. Too bad they don't make something like that for men."

"Guess we have to stick with the flask," Hank agreed, his lips twitching.

"Please don't think my daughter, your future daughter-in-law, is a lush," Mom said primly. "It's just the wild influence of her great-aunt."

Bernadette laughed. "I've heard of the grand adventures of Ryli and Aunt Shirley. I can't wait to hear more later on."

Aunt Shirley grinned at Bernadette. "I have plenty of stories to share. Clear back from my time living in Hollywood and dating the stars all the way up until now. Did Ace here tell you someone is trying to murder me this week?"

Bernadette glanced over at Garrett and then smiled weakly at Aunt Shirley. "Um, no he didn't."

Aunt Shirley nodded. "Yep. Already killed two people I know this week, keeps leaving me cryptic notes, and has now promised to kill me within…" Aunt Shirley trailed off and furrowed her brow. "I guess he's promised to kill me within the next twenty-four hours."

Bernadette gasped. "Should we be having this wedding?"

"Yes!" the whole kitchen shouted.

Mom laughed self-consciously. "What we mean to say is that if we waited until Aunt Shirley and Ryli were safe before Garrett and Ryli married…well, they'd never get married because those two are always stumbling over bodies and being chased by murderers."

Bernadette's mouth dropped open. "Always?"

I rolled my eyes. "Gee, Mom, thanks."

Mom bit her lip. "Well, you know what I mean. Right, Garrett?"

Garrett chuckled and threw his hands up. "I'm staying out of this one."

I shot him an evil look.

He walked over and kissed me hard on the lips. "You look beautiful."

"Don't try and change the subject," I whispered against his mouth.

He gave me a much longer kiss and everyone clapped and hollered.

"Let's go get you two pretend married," Hank said.

Mom led the way outside to the fenced-in backyard. Even though Mom lived in town, she lived on one acre, so there would be plenty of room for the guests to mingle tomorrow night. My breath caught as I lifted the bottom of my black, long-sleeved sheath dress and walked down the deck steps and onto the grassy area where we would be married. There were a handful of chairs on each side of the aisle that stopped in front of a small pergola that Garrett and Matt had built during their down time.

The back half of the yard sported a huge tent with about twenty tables underneath. Each tabletop was decorated in burlap, lace, and hurricanes with candles. A medium-sized, wooden dancefloor was off to the right of the yard, near the fence. Mason jars with candles hung from nearly every branch of every tree would be lit for the ceremony tomorrow night.

"It's beautiful, Mom," I sniffed. Like always, Mom had pulled through. And like always, doubt flooded me.

"We'll be right there," Garrett said to the crowd. "Give us just a few minutes, please."

The rest of the party headed over to the seats. I could tell they were curious what was going on but were too polite to ask.

I took a deep breath and turned to Garrett.

"Don't even say anything," Garrett said. "I can tell by the look on your face you're about to bolt."

I let out a hysterical giggle.

Garrett gathered my hands in his. "Ryli, stop doubting yourself. That's exactly what you're doing right now. I don't know why you're always comparing yourself to others around you, but you do."

"You have no idea what it's like to grow up with a mother that's nearly perfect in everything she does. Even Paige and Aunt Shirley have things they excel in. I really don't have that, Garrett. You're marrying a woman who can barely cook a meal. I dump all the laundry into one huge pile and wash it. I wouldn't even know how to separate the clothes if you asked me to. I don't know—"

Garrett put a finger up to my lips. "Stop. Just stop. It's annoying when you feel the need to list your shortcomings to me. Like what? You don't think I don't already know all this stuff about you?" He chuckled. "Ryli, I know you're a hot mess. It's kinda one of the things I love most about you. I'd be a fool if I thought by marrying me tomorrow you would somehow turn into the perfect wife. And that's *your* definition of perfect, not mine."

"I just want you to be proud of who I am, and I don't know what I can do to make that happen."

"I'm very proud of who you are, Ryli. In fact, if anyone should apologize for shortcomings, it's me. I've been an idiot this last year, hounding you about your safety and harassing you about pursuing a career you are good at and capable of. Mainly because I'm afraid of losing you." He gave me a sly smile. "I was going to save this surprise for tomorrow, but I think now is the perfect time."

He dug into his pocket and took out a piece of paper and handed it to me. I carefully unfolded the paper and began to read— my eyes growing wide when I realized what it was.

126

"Is this what I think it is?" I asked.

Garrett smiled. "It is. I purchased your entrance ticket to take the PI exam."

I let out a whoop and threw my arms around him. "Oh, Garret! Thank you!"

He drew me back and gave me a hard kiss. "I'm very proud of you, Ryli Jo Sinclair. Never doubt that. All these little things you're worrying about, they don't matter. What matters is that we love each other, we respect each other, and we know how to hold each other up in good and bad times." He wiped the tears off my cheeks. "And I figured this was the best way for me to show you how proud I am of you and how much I want this for you."

"I love you, Garrett."

"And I love you, Sin."

We kissed again and I felt like I could burst with happiness.

"Ahem!" Aunt Shirley called out. "Are we gonna get this show on the road, or are we gonna have to watch you two make out all night?"

"I'd give her lip back," I whispered against Garrett's mouth, "but I'm kinda scared of her in that ridiculous getup. She looks like a Goth witch who ate a princess. I bet you just can't *wait* to marry into this family."

Garrett chuckled against my mouth. "Let's go get pretend married."

CHAPTER 17

"How's the bride this morning?" Aunt Shirley asked as I lumbered into the kitchen the next morning around ten o'clock.

I groaned. "Maybe I should have stopped after three glasses of wine."

"*And* laid off the boozy bracelet I gave you," Aunt Shirley cackled.

After the rehearsal, I ate, drank, and talked late into the night. Garrett and Matt were still technically on duty, so the drinking was left to the rest of us. By the time Garrett made it back over to drive his parents out to his place, everyone was having a great time. Although in the back of my mind I couldn't help but worry about when the next shoe would drop. When would Danner strike next?

Garrett had texted late last night and said he'd heard from a deputy that all was quiet out at the Kealey place. Danner had not come back as of eleven o'clock last night. Garrett said he didn't feel he would, either. Danner had found a new place to hide.

Mom plopped down a plate in front of me. "French toast with homemade whipped cream. That should help."

My mouth watered just looking at the whipped cream beginning to melt onto the hot French toast. "Thanks, Mom."

"Hot tea or coffee?" Mindy asked from her station at the counter.

I chuckled. "It's a coffee morning for me."

"Morning everyone," Paige greeted jovially as she lowered herself into a chair.

"Not so loud," I mumbled around a forkful of French toast.

Paige grinned. "Are you not feeling so good this morning? I wonder why?"

I glared at her. "Just because you can't drink doesn't mean you need to rub it in."

Paige snorted. "That's *exactly* what that means."

"Decaf herbal tea for you," Mindy said as she set a cup in front of Paige.

"We're all ready to go," Mom said. "The caterers will get here around four to set up. Flowers arrive at three, and the cake, cupcakes, and cookies will be right around that time, too. Mindy and I are going to start making up the igloos of margaritas in a little while."

I stood up and gave Mom a hug and kiss. "Thanks. You're the best for taking care of all this stuff."

Mom laughed. "That's because I knew if I wanted a nice wedding I was gonna have to design it."

I shrugged. "True."

I finished off the French toast and took a huge gulp of my strong, black coffee. I was beginning to feel much better.

"What are you going to do today?" Paige asked.

I looked at Aunt Shirley. "Mainly we're all sticking together. No one goes anywhere alone. We don't leave each other's sides today."

We all nodded in agreement.

"I'm going upstairs to do a facial, then take a little nap, then I'm going to start getting ready around two," I said. "That should give me plenty of time to be ready by five."

Aunt Shirley snorted. "I should hope so."

I gave her my best death stare. "This is my big day, and I'm going to make sure I look like I'm a confident woman ready to marry the Chief of Police."

Mindy lifted her herbal tea in the air. "I say we all drink to that."

We clinked our coffee and tea mugs together in laughter. If only I could squelch the thought that the worst was yet to come.

***

"How're we doing on time?" I asked as I got out of Mom's Jacuzzi tub.

Paige laughed. "It's two o'clock. You're right where you said you wanted to be by this time."

I wrapped a towel around my body and looked at myself in the mirror. Paige scooted a mug my way. "I had your mom put a splash of brandy in it for you."

I rested my hands on my stomach. "Is it that obvious?"

Paige nodded. "Yeah. You've had this terrified look on your face for about thirty minutes now.

"I thought the bath would help."

I heard Aunt Shirley yelling from downstairs and opened the bathroom door. The shrieking was so loud, for a minute I thought she was standing outside the door. Paige and I rushed to the top of the stairs to listen in.

"I told that man no one leaves alone!" Aunt Shirley screamed. "How could you let him leave here alone?"

"He's a full-grown man," Hank grumbled. "He said he'd be right back."

"How long?" Aunt Shirley demanded. "How long has he been gone?"

"About forty minutes," Doc said.

"What's going on?" I hollered down from the top of the stairs.

Aunt Shirley stalked over and looked up at me. "Get dressed. The old man evidently got a phone call about forty minutes ago from our floor orderly, Libby, saying there was an emergency in our apartment. And like an idiot he just ran over there."

My heart dropped and I grabbed onto the banister.

"Get dressed," Aunt Shirley snapped. "We leave in two minutes!"

"I'll go get him," Hank said. "If you're really that worried."

"No one's going anywhere," Mom said as she rushed into the foyer. "Let Garrett handle this. Ryli, you continue getting ready for your wedding."

I looked over at Aunt Shirley. She looked pale and worried.

"No, Mom. I'm going to go get dressed and Aunt Shirley and I will run really quick to the Manor. I promise we won't be long."

Mom sighed and threw her hands up. "I *knew* it would be too much to ask for the day to go smoothly."

"Mom," I said as calmly as I could, "Aunt Shirley needs us right now."

Mom looked at Aunt Shirley for the first time since entering the room.

"Go get dressed, Ryli," Mom said quietly. "Be down here in two minutes."

I bolted down the hallway, tossed my towel onto the bedroom floor, and shoved my legs into a pair of black yoga pants. I wrestled my wet body into a sports bra and threw on a sweatshirt over the bra. Yanking open a drawer I took out the first pair of socks I found and bent down to put them on.

"Here." Paige handed me a rubber band. "Tie your hair back so it doesn't dry funny."

I smiled tightly at her and did as she requested. I leaned over and gave her a quick kiss and took off down the stairs as fast as my socked feet would safely allow. I slid into the kitchen and grabbed onto the counter to keep from falling.

"I need to put my shoes on and I'm ready," I said to no one in particular.

Aunt Shirley was shoving her gun, nunchucks, and ninja stars in her purse, ignoring Hank's yelling.

"You want to call Garrett, fine," Aunt Shirley snapped as she stood up. "I'm not wasting the time. Ryli, let's go."

Mom grabbed me by the arm and gave me a kiss. "Be safe, please."

"We will," I vowed. "I promise."

I looked over at Hank. He was already digging out his cell phone.

I quickly tied my laces and sprinted out the door behind Aunt Shirley. The minute the Falcon turned over, I put it in reverse and peeled out of the drive. I hadn't even gotten to the end of the street before my cell rang.

"It's Garrett," I said, recognizing the ring tone.

Aunt Shirley took the phone from me, her hands visibly shaking.

"We're heading to the Manor right now," Aunt Shirley said by way of greeting.

I could hear Garrett talking but couldn't make out the words.

"Don't you give me no grief, Garrett Kimble. This is my husband we're talking about. I'll meet you there." Aunt Shirley hit the end button and tossed my phone in her purse.

Oh, boy…not the start of my wedding day I was planning.

I skidded into the circle drive at the Manor and put the Falcon in park. Aunt Shirley and I jumped out and ran to the door just as Garrett was pulling up.

"You can't park out there," the orderly behind the information desk shouted to us.

"Police business," Garrett said as he rushed past Aunt Shirley and me. "I'll get the elevator."

Aunt Shirley and I paused to catch our breath as the elevator dinged and the doors slid open. We all rushed on and Garrett pressed the closed button repeatedly.

"Let me go in first." He said it in a way that left us no room to argue.

Aunt Shirley closed her eyes and nodded her head.

The elevator doors opened and Garrett rushed out, weapon drawn.

"Please, Lord," Aunt Shirley whispered, "don't let him be dead."

I grabbed hold of her hand and squeezed it. I wanted to scream at Old Man Jenkins and ask him what the heck he thought he was doing! Instead, I took a deep breath and leaned against the wall like Garrett motioned me to do.

He threw open the door and then flattened himself against the wall next to me. I could hear muffled screaming coming from inside the apartment.

"Wait here until I say it's clear," Garrett demanded.

I nodded.

His gun up, he flew around the corner and into the apartment. More muffled screams. I looked at Aunt Shirley. She had a death grip on her purse, but no weapons were out.

"Clear!" Garrett yelled.

Aunt Shirley and I dashed into the apartment. Libby, the orderly in charge of the second floor, was tied up and gagged.

Garrett yanked the tape off her mouth in one fluid motion. More screams of pain filled the air. He then went to work on her ties.

"Where's Waylon?" Aunt Shirley demanded.

Libby started to cry as she talked. No one understood a word she said.

"Hold on," Garrett said. "I need you to take a deep breath and try again. I don't mean to pressure you, Libby, but I need you to pull yourself together and tell me what I need to know."

Libby nodded and took a deep breath. "I was making my rounds on the second floor when someone jumped me and dragged me into the janitor's closet right across the hall. He had a kn-kn-knife and…" she trailed off, her teeth chattering from shock.

Garrett covered her hands with his. "Deep breath. So he dragged you into the closet, put a knife to your throat, and then what?"

134

Libby nodded and took another deep breath. "Then he told me I was going to call Mr. Jenkins's cell phone and tell him I was going to be ki-ki-killed if he didn't get over here immediately. And alone. He was to come alone."

I looked over at the floor and my blood went cold. "Oh, crap. Whose blood, Libby?"

Aunt Shirley whimpered and her hands flew up to cover her mouth.

"I don't know," Libby whispered. "I actually think it might be the bad guy's blood. When Mr. Jenkins came through the door, the guy was hiding behind it and he hit Mr. Jenkins over the head with his knife, but Mr. Jenkins didn't go down."

"That sounds about right," Aunt Shirley agreed as she wiped tears off her cheeks. "He's one hard-headed man."

I smiled, relieved Aunt Shirley could at least crack a joke.

"Mr. Jenkins spun around, blood dripping from his head, and he sprang at the bad guy. The two of them fell on the floor, wrestling over the knife. I heard the bad guy cry out in pain once, but then everything stopped suddenly when a gun flew out of Mr. Jenkins's hand."

"He must have brought his .38 with him," Aunt Shirley said, her voice stronger now.

"The bad guy staggered to his feet, blood flowing from his side, waved the knife around and told Mr. Jenkins they were going for a little ride." Libby bit her lip and whimpered. "The bad guy picked up the gun, came over to me and ran the knife over my face and told me I was supposed to tell Mrs. Jenkins that she dug this hole for her husband."

For once Aunt Shirley didn't correct the girl when she called her Mrs. Jenkins.

"He said to tell me that I dug this hole?" Aunt Shirley demanded.

"Yes," Libby said.

"What the hell is it with these stupid cryptic messages?" Aunt Shirley shouted.

CHAPTER 18

"Here's what we're gonna do," Garrett said. "Ryli, do you have all the messages written down somewhere? If not, go to the station and look them over."

I dug my cell phone out of my bra. "I have them stored on my phone."

"Good. I've gone over them and I believe Danner is referencing a cemetery. Read over them and tell me what you think. Now, I think this has been Danner's plan all along and he's taken Jenkins to a cemetery. There are two in the city limits of Granville, and three outside of the city limits. I'm going to have the sheriff cover the country cemeteries."

"What will you do?" Aunt Shirley demanded.

"I'm going to have Officer Ryan escort my parents to Janine's house. I don't want them out in the open. Matt and I will process the scene here as quickly as we can. If we can prove this blood is Danner's, we will have us a manhunt. The FBI will be involved. We'll have a lot more help to get Danner before he—" Garrett stopped and took a deep breath. "Before he has a chance to hurt Jenkins."

I nodded "You got it. Aunt Shirley and I will look over the messages and see if we come up with the same conclusion as you."

I grabbed Aunt Shirley's sleeve and started to haul her out the door.

"Ryli!"

I turned and watched in amazement as Garrett grabbed hold of my face and gave me a hard kiss. "Please be careful. Keep your phone on and call me the instant you have something on the code. Or call me the instant something happens. Understand?"

I smiled up at him. If it were a different occasion, I'd be overjoyed at the thought Garrett was finally letting me help him. But I couldn't bring myself to feel joy when Old Man Jenkins was probably hurt and in the hands of a vicious killer. "Understood. I'll keep you abreast of any changes."

Aunt Shirley and I flew down the hallway to the elevator. As we waited impatiently for the elevator to open, I clicked on my phone and pulled up the notes. "You got a piece of paper in that enormous purse of yours?"

Aunt Shirley nodded. "You read them to me and I'll write them down again."

We hurried over to an empty table in the lobby.

"The first one says, 'I hear congratulations are in order. I hope this marriage isn't a grave mistake.' Then there was the note he left in your apartment with the knife through the pumpkin that said, 'Don't you think it's time we bury the hatchet?' And then there was the one at Lucy's place that said, 'I wish that just once people wouldn't act like the clichés they are—Six Feet Under.' And then the last interaction was basically him saying someone you loved would die within the next two days. Plus we have Libby's statement that Danner said you dug this hole yourself." I swallowed past the lump in my throat at the thought of Old Man Jenkins being kidnapped.

"First things first," Aunt Shirley said. "This six feet under thing. What do you think that means?"

"Well, six feet under is usually a reference to how far down a casket is buried." I pulled up the internet on my cell phone and typed in 'six feet under.' "Well, now this is interesting."

"What?" Aunt Shirley demanded.

"*Six Feet Under* was a television show years ago. So I definitely think Garrett's right. Words like 'bury' and 'grave' and now the *Six Feet Under* reference, I think Danner is holding Old Man Jenkins somewhere in a cemetery."

"But which one, dammit!" Aunt Shirley exclaimed. "I figured it was a cemetery, but I thought the clues might lead us to which *one* it was."

I sucked in my breath. "That cow! If she's involved, I'll kill her myself!"

"What?" Aunt Shirley demanded.

"Let's go!"

We fled out of the Manor like the Devil himself was chasing us. I slid over the top of the Falcon's hood, righted myself, and plopped down inside. My hands were shaking so badly, it took me two tries to jam the key into the ignition. I leaned back up, floored the gas pedal, and peeled out of the circle drive, fishtailing the whole way out.

"Good Lord, girl. Where are we going?"

My fingers tightened on the steering wheel. "I think I might know who's involved."

"Who?"

I turned onto the main drag and headed to Quilter's Paradise. "Do you remember the other day when Willa said under her breath that it was Garrett's funeral? Well, don't you think it's odd that she did that? I mean, of all the things she could have said she picks a funeral word when we're dealing with cemetery and funeral words? And what's the deal with this new guy her mom is suddenly seeing? How many new guys do you know come into town?"

Aunt Shirley scrunched her forehead. "Wait. Are you thinking the new guy Phoebe Trindle is seeing is Danner? How would that have even happened? That's kind of a huge leap, don't you think?"

I jerked the wheel to the left and we slid sideways into the parking lot of Quilter's Paradise. "Heck no I don't! I think it's time Willa and I had a little heart-to-heart chat."

I jumped out of the Falcon and cracked my neck and rolled my shoulders. "Time for a Willa beat-down! By the time I'm done with her, we'll have Old Man Jenkins's whereabouts known."

Not waiting for Aunt Shirley, I sprinted for the front door of the store and threw it open with more force than I meant to. Luckily no one was standing near the door or I would have knocked them out cold.

"Slow your roll there, cupcake," Aunt Shirley said dryly. "I'm still not sure about this."

But it was like I didn't hear her.

I saw Willa behind the cash register and took off for her. Her eyes went huge and she let out a cry when she saw me charging straight for her. I reached out and grabbed her around the throat by her shirt collar then yanked her down to my eye level.

"Where is he?" I snarled.

She let out another startled scream and brought her arms up to push me away.

I gave her another shake for good measure. "Where is he? I won't ask again. If I have to beat it out of you, I will!"

"What's going on here?"

I turned and saw Bonnie Macario's mouth hanging open. Her cart was full of supplies and it looked like she was ready to check out.

"Hey, Bonnie," I said as pleasantly as I could. "This shouldn't take but a minute."

I turned back to Willa. "I know you're involved with Old Man Jenkins's disappearance and the murder of Lucy Stevenson and Miss Mabel."

Willa's face grew pale. "What are you talking about? Have you totally lost your mind?"

"The man your mom is hooking up with is Nicholas Wayne Danner, known serial killer and rapist."

Bonnie gasped.

I ignored Bonnie and went on. "And now Danner has Old Man Jenkins. And if you don't tell me where Danner has taken him, I will beat you to within an inch of your life!"

"I don't know what you're talking about!" Willa cried. "The man my mom is seeing isn't this Nicholas Danner guy!"

Aunt Shirley put a hand on my arm. "Ryli, maybe we should take this somewhere else. We got us a crowd gathering."

I didn't spare a glance. "We're gonna end this right here."

Willa's nose started to run as she burst into tears. "The guy my mom's bringing is my uncle! Okay. It's my uncle. Her brother that lives in Iowa." Willa continued to blubber and cry harder. "Mom was just trying to make everyone jealous and say she has a new guy. It's my uncle. He's not a killer."

I sobered instantly at the confession, but my mind was having a hard time back pedaling.

Dang! I was so sure about this!

"So you don't know anything about Old Man Jenkins's disappearance?" I asked. I could hear the desperation in my voice. I thought for sure I had it figured out.

"No! I don't!"

"Is everything okay?" Blair Watkins asked as she made her way toward the checkout counter.

I released my hold on Willa's throat and stepped back.

"Everything's fine," Aunt Shirley said. "Just a little pre-wedding jitters is all."

Blair looked at Willa, then me, then Willa again. "Willa, are you okay?"

Willa nodded but refused to look at me.

"Just a misunderstanding," I said.

"C'mon, Ryli, we need to get out of here and find my husband."

Aunt Shirley and I raced back to the Falcon and I revved up the engine.

"Why did you think Danner and this mystery guy were one in the same?" Aunt Shirley asked. "Or why Willa was involved?"

"Her saying the words 'it's his funeral' and then going on about a mystery guy her mom met online. I thought maybe somehow Danner started up an online love tryst with Mrs. Trindle."

"Blech!" Aunt Shirley said. "But I guess I can see how you drew that assumption."

I rested my head on the steering wheel and groaned. "Think Willa will press charges?"

Aunt Shirley chuckled. "What's she gonna do? Get Garrett to arrest you? No, I think she's more embarrassed than anything."

I sighed and lifted my dejected head up off the wheel. "Where to now?"

"I think we check in with Garrett."

"I wish I had my gun," I said. "I feel stupid not carrying it."

"I have this for you." Aunt Shirley took out a black, medium-sized gun from her purse. "Hank gave it to me before we headed out. Just in case. It's a SIG."

"A what?"

"SIG," Aunt Shirley repeated. "Broken down it's a pistol."

"Got it. Now, let's go find your husband and the man that's going to walk me down the aisle."

CHAPTER 19

Without another word, Aunt Shirley grabbed her cell phone, pushed a button, and spoke into it. "Ryli and I agree he's taken Waylon to a cemetery." The raw emotion made Aunt Shirley's voice raspy and dry. "Where do you want us to go?"

I could vaguely make out Garrett's voice.

"Copy that. We'll meet you there."

"What's next?" I asked the minute she hung up.

"Officer Ryan and Matt are going to the cemetery off Park Lane here in town, and Garrett wants you, me, and Hank to meet at the cemetery by the old grain bin. He said the sheriff and a couple deputies are patrolling the country cemeteries, but no sightings as of yet."

"Do you think Mom and everyone will be safe if Hank leaves them at the house alone?"

Aunt Shirley nodded. "Garrett's parents are at your Mom's, and they took a lot of weapons from Garrett's house before they left. Your Glock included."

I breathed a sigh of relief. I really didn't want to try and handle Hank's SIG. I made a left on Oak Street and slowed the Falcon down a little. The old grain bin was on a road that was mostly gravel. I didn't want the dust to give me away.

I looked in my rear-view mirror and saw Hank's Jeep barreling down on my backend. So much for inconspicuous. I pushed down on the gas pedal and sped up so Hank wouldn't run me off the road.

I flew past the grain bin and took the next right. The arched, wrought iron sign announced Mt. Olivet Cemetery. I turned down the narrow, gravel and grass path and kept driving. Mt. Olivet Cemetery was surrounded by a dense thicket of trees on all sides. The cemetery was basically situated on a large square. Once you got to the start of the graves, you could continue straight through, or branch off and go either right or left.

I didn't have to worry which direction to go because I saw Garrett's patrol truck positioned behind the right half of the mausoleum. Garrett motioned from inside his truck for me to park next to him so I was completely protected behind the mausoleum, while Hank pulled up and was partially covered by the left half of the mausoleum. Hank and Garrett both got out of their vehicles, surveying the area around them.

"I called in a favor," Garrett said. "Local guy I know has his pilot's license and access to a plane, so he just did a flyby for me. He said he saw a blue car over that little ridge past the last row of graves. I radioed Matt and Officer Ryan for backup. I also called for an ambulance. I want them stationed right outside the cemetery's entrance. No sense making Danner any jumpier than he probably already is."

"What's the game plan?" Hank asked.

"First off, I ran by the station and grabbed a couple vests," Garrett said. "I want Ryli and Aunt Shirley to buckle up. I'm worried since Danner has nothing to lose he'll call Aunt Shirley out. I want to make sure she's protected as much as possible."

I counted to ten so I wouldn't hyperventilate. I'd be lying if I said I wasn't scared...but I also knew Aunt Shirley was right, I couldn't let my fear show. This was my first do or die moment with Garrett, and I wanted to prove to him I could do this.

Garrett threw the vests at Aunt Shirley and me and we quickly shed our sweatshirts and donned the vests. Or at least I tried to quickly don the vest. It fit so tight my breasts were flattened against me, and I was having a difficult time breathing. Garrett Velcroed my sides together. I now knew what a sausage felt like.

"This is worse than wearing Spanx," I gasped.

"You got that right," Aunt Shirley agreed. "My girls will probably never be the same."

Garrett groaned. "Let's not go there. Lift your arms and I'll help you two get your sweatshirts back on."

"Here." Hank handed me my Glock once I was fully dressed again. "I'll take back the SIG."

Garrett lifted the corner of his mouth. "You gave her your SIG to shoot?"

Hank shrugged. "Of all the guns I brought with me to Janine's house, I figured that would be the easiest for her."

Geez, I'd hate to see what his other guns looked like.

I heard the purr of an engine and caught Matt and Officer Ryan creeping toward us in a patrol car. They parked behind Hank's Jeep and cautiously made their way toward us.

"We passed the ambulance coming in," Matt said. "Everyone should be in position now."

Garrett nodded. "Good. Now let me fill you in on the rest of the plan."

146

By the time Garrett finished talking, I was so scared I could hardly breathe. If any one little thing went wrong, it meant instant death for Aunt Shirley...and maybe even Old Man Jenkins.

Everyone crept to their locations and Garrett grabbed his bullhorn out of the truck and walked to the front of the mausoleum. Aunt Shirley and I were to crouch behind Hank's Jeep until Garrett told us otherwise. I grabbed Aunt Shirley's hand and held on for dear life. She squeezed back, but I could tell she was just as terrified.

"Danner," Garrett squawked through the bullhorn, "we know you're here. C'mon out and bring Jenkins with you. We want proof he's still alive."

Silence.

I glanced at Aunt Shirley's pale face, but she ignored me.

"Danner?" Garrett called again.

"I'm coming up," Danner yelled. "I got the old man with me, so don't shoot unless you want to kill him."

I peeked around Hank's Jeep, and after what seemed like ten minutes, but was really only ten seconds, I saw two heads crest the top of the ridge. A few more tense seconds later and Old Man Jenkins—Danner directly behind him—came to a limping stop out in the open. Danner had his left arm around Old Man Jenkins's upper torso and throat, but the gun in Danner's right hand kept wavering between Jenkins's head and side, like the gun was too heavy for Danner to lift. I could see from my vantage point the dried blood on the side of Old Man Jenkins's face where Danner had hit him when he first entered the apartment a while back. Other than that, Jenkins looked to be doing okay.

Danner on the other hand looked like death. Between his obvious sickness dealing with the cancer, and the stab wound he reportedly undertook, he was struggling just to stay on his feet. The blood oozing from his left side made me think Libby had been right when she said she thought Danner had been wounded in the struggle between the two men.

"Looks like Danner's wounded," Aunt Shirley whispered. "He's having a hard time keeping Waylon in front of him and the gun lifted to his head. That should be a bonus for us."

"You got to see the old man," Danner grunted through pinched lips, "now I wanna see the bitch that put me away for all these years."

I gasped. Even though I knew what was coming, I was still afraid for Aunt Shirley. If it didn't play out exactly as it needed to, the whole thing could go south. And rarely did our endings go as planned.

Aunt Shirley stood up and slowly made her way past the Jeep, then past the mausoleum, until she was out in the open, about ten yards from where Danner and Old Man Jenkins were standing. Her back was ramrod straight.

"Shirley Andrews, as I live and breathe," Danner said snidely. "Oh, wait, it's not Andrews anymore is it? It's Jenkins now. Sorry I missed the big day."

I couldn't see Aunt Shirley's face, so I couldn't tell what she was feeling or how his words were affecting her.

"Danner," Aunt Shirley ground out. "Wish I could say it's nice to see you…but we both know that would be a lie."

Danner lifted the gun up to Old Man Jenkins's head. "Watch your tongue, hag, or your lover here gets it."

"Now, Danner, you and I both know you aren't going to shoot him that quickly. Where would the fun in that be?"

Danner laughed darkly. "Guess you're right. I just wish I had the time to cut you both up like you deserve."

Danner winced and lowered the gun to Old Man Jenkins's side again. "Your damn husband nicked me with my own blade. So I guess it's fitting I kill you both with his own gun." Danner attempted to laugh but ended up in a coughing fit.

"Let's get this over with," Aunt Shirley said once Danner was done coughing and he'd lowered the gun again. "You know these three policemen behind me aren't going to let you just shoot both me and Waylon. You're gonna have to choose which one of us you shoot."

Danner cut his eyes up to where Garrett, Matt, and Officer Ryan were standing stalwart in front of the mausoleum. "I have to say, they don't look all that concerned about you, Shirley. Why is that? Do they know you so well they probably won't be too sad to see your nosey, interfering ass sprawled out dead on the ground?"

Danner started to laugh again, his guard momentarily down, when a shot rang out.

Bang!

Aunt Shirley cried out, staggered forward a half an inch before falling face first into the ground.

I screamed.

Even though I knew it was coming…I screamed. The sound of the gun and seeing Aunt Shirley pitch forward was too much for me to bear.

"Get down," I finally remembered to scream at Old Man Jenkins.

Old Man Jenkins dropped like a sack of potatoes.

"What the—"

Danner never got to finish his sentence. By the time he realized Aunt Shirley had been shot, and his human shield—Old Man Jenkins—was on the ground, he barely had enough time to lift his gun to shoot.

Who he intended to shoot, I don't know. Aunt Shirley who was already on the ground? Old Man Jenkins who was also on the ground? Garrett? Or maybe even himself? I have no idea and I'll never know.

Because the minute Danner lifted his gun to shoot, Garrett put a bullet between his eyes.

CHAPTER 20

"Aunt Shirley!" I screamed as I sprang up off the ground and raced to her prone body.

Garrett, Matt, and Officer Ryan followed close on my heels. Garrett, Matt, and I gathered around Aunt Shirley while Officer Ryan went to make sure Danner was secure. And by secure...I mean good and dead.

"I'll call it in and get the ambulance out here," Officer Ryan said.

"I'm cool," Aunt Shirley said as she struggled to stand up on her own.

"Let me help you up," Garrett reached out and steadied Aunt Shirley before glancing back at Old Man Jenkins. "You okay back there, Jenkins?"

"Dagnabbit, is my wife dead?" Old Man Jenkins hollered out as he struggled to get his eighty-five-year-old feet under him. "Is she dead? And who the hell shot her?"

"I'm okay you fool," Aunt Shirley called out. "I was shot on purpose. And I'm not speaking to you right now, you old ornery cuss. What the heck were you thinking running off alone like that when you know darn good and well that—"

"How much bellyaching are you planning on doing?" Old Man Jenkins asked as he walked into our circle. "Because if it's much more, maybe I'll go see if Danner left any bullets in my gun and put myself out of my own misery!"

My mouth dropped open and a giggle escaped. I clamped my hand over my mouth to keep the hysterical laughter to a minimum.

"Nice shot," Aunt Shirley said as Hank lumbered over and joined the circle.

"You shot my wife?" Old Man Jenkins ask incredulously.

Hank grinned. "I sure did. And I enjoyed every minute of it!"

Aunt Shirley gave Garret the evil eye. "Well, it hurt a lot worse than I expected it to. I think you gave me a defective vest."

Garrett smiled. "I got them on sale. Guess now I know why."

I gasped.

Garrett chuckled. "I'm joking, Ryli."

The ambulance wail broke the mood as reality came crashing back to us. Danner was dead...but not after murdering two Granville citizens and terrorizing multiple families.

"I called out the coroner," Office Ryan said.

"Thanks," Garrett answered.

"I'll bring the EMTs over here so they can look at Jenkins." Matt took off at a jog to wave over the EMTs.

Old Man Jenkins put a wrinkled, shaking hand to his temple. "Got me a little bit of a headache."

"Oh, you old fool," Aunt Shirley said as she surreptitiously wiped her eyes. "Let me see."

"I'm fine! You ain't no doctor," Old Man Jenkins grumbled. "I mean, you got the bedside manner of a doctor, but you ain't one!"

Hank chuckled and walked back toward his Jeep. "Gonna go secure my weapon."

"I better call Mom and tell her we're okay." I walked back toward the Falcon, shucking my sweatshirt and then my bullet-proof vest. Glad I could finally breathe again, I tugged the sweatshirt back on and then took out my cell phone.

I yanked open the driver's side door, slid behind the wheel, and dropped the phone next to me. I felt the sobs rising and figured there was no sense trying to stifle them. I laid my head down on the steering wheel and sobbed. I cried for Old Man Jenkins, I cried for Lucy and Miss Mabel, I cried for Aunt Shirley, and I cried even harder when I realized I was supposed to be married to the man I love in an hour and a half.

The passenger door opened and Garrett sat down. "Can anyone join your party or is it invitation only?"

I managed a watery laugh…then started crying again.

"C'mere." Garrett gathered me in his arms and held my head against his chest. "It breaks my heart when you cry, Ryli."

I swiped at my nose. "I can't help it. I kn-know I'm supposed to be st-st-strong, but seeing Aunt Shirley get shot and Old Man Jenkins bleeding. I don't kn-know if I'm cut out for this."

Garrett chuckled. "Honey, those are just the endorphins talking. Your body is just coming down from a shock. It happens to us all."

"Does it?" I whispered.

"Yes." He pushed me away from him and cupped my cheek. "Ryli, you are plenty strong and plenty capable." He brushed his lips across mine then smacked his lips together. "Salty."

I laughed and wiped my face. "Go away. I think technically you aren't supposed to see me before the wedding."

"Ah…the wedding." Garrett winked. "I think we can have this wrapped up in about an hour. Gives me half an hour to spare before I marry the woman I love."

"Oh, great. You're gonna look fabulous, and I'm going to look like a puffy chipmunk."

Garrett kissed my nose. "Chipmunks are cute. Call your mom, tell her you'll be home in twenty minutes. We can deal with paperwork later."

"Okay."

"And, Ryli, you know you could walk down that aisle in yoga pants and your hair in a bun and I'd still think you're the hottest thing around for miles."

My face broke out in a grin. "You don't have to sweet talk me. You're pretty much guaranteed to get lucky tonight."

"That's my girl!"

***

By the time the puffiness left my face and I got my hair and makeup done, it was a little after five. The wedding would only be a few minutes late. Paige was helping me wiggle into my wedding dress when Mom entered my bedroom carrying the veil.

"Oh, honey." Mom's eyes welled up with tears and her lower lip trembled.

"Don't cry!" I shouted. "Your face will get puffy. I'll start crying and *my* face will get puffy...and we'll look like puffer fish in the photos!"

Mom laughed and blinked back the tears. "You're right. I can do this."

"She does look beautiful, doesn't she?" Paige declared. She stepped back and let Mom secure my veil. But not before I saw Paige wince.

"You okay?" I asked.

Paige waved her hand. "I'm fine. I think the twins have hiccups."

I frowned and stared harder at her.

"I'm serious!" Paige said. "I'm perfectly fine. I mean, I'm the size of a barn, but I feel fine."

The door flew open and Aunt Shirley lumbered in. "Speaking of barns, did you have to make my dress the color of one?"

I rolled my eyes. "Your dress is burgundy."

Aunt Shirley glowered at Paige. "Why did she get to wear the dark purple dress? Purple is royalty. I should wear the purple dress."

I laughed sardonically. "You get the burgundy because it's named after wine. You're the lush of the group…I found burgundy fitting for you."

Aunt Shirley beamed. "Hey, I like that!"

I rolled my eyes again and shook my head.

"Hold still, honey," Mom said. "I'm almost done. Okay, there."

Mom took a step back and let me see myself in the mirror.

A collective gasp went up. I have to say, I looked stunning.

My wedding dress was a floor-length ball gown with a lace bodice and off-the-shoulder cap sleeves. I reached up and touched the sweetheart neckline then ran my hand down to the cinched waist. "The tulle is what really makes this dress," I whispered. The bottom of the dress was completely made of tulle. "I love everything about this dress."

"It almost looks like the dress I wore last night," Aunt Shirley said.

I laughed. "No. It doesn't. It doesn't look *anything* like your Goth creation from last night." I turned sideways in the mirror. "And the veil is magnificent."

"Yes, it is," Mom agreed.

"I think I'm ready," I said.

Paige sighed. "I can't believe how much our lives have changed over the past year."

I smiled weakly. "I was just saying that the other day. I almost wish it would slow down again."

Mom pressed her forehead to mine. "And the best is yet to come for you, Ryli Jo."

A knock on the door made us all jump.

"You ready in there?" Doc asked.

"We don't want to keep the guests waiting," Old Man Jenkins added. The EMTs had declared Old Man Jenkins to have a mild concussion, but he said nothing was going to keep him from helping Doc walk me down the aisle.

"Garrett, Matt, and Officer Ryan just lined up." Doc said, giving us a play-by-play now.

I giggled. "Do you suppose there will ever come a time when we finally call Officer Ryan by his first name."

Paige shook her head. "No way. That man scares me to death. He'll always be Officer Ryan."

Mom picked my bouquet of flowers off the bed. "Let's go get you married, Ryli."

CHAPTER 21

"Are you ready?" Doc looped his arm through my left arm as we stood out on the back deck.

I closed my eyes and inhaled deeply. This was it. I was about to walk down the aisle and become Mrs. Ryli Kimble.

"You look beautiful, my dear." Old Man Jenkins threaded his arm through my right arm.

I opened my eyes and blinked back tears. The backyard was illuminated in soft, flickering white lights. Myriad candles shimmered in jars hanging from the nearly-bare trees, and the white Christmas lights surrounding the perimeter of the fence and encircling the pergola made me feel like I was about to step into a fairy tale.

I glanced at each man at my side. "I'm ready."

Mindy saw my nod and pushed a button on her phone. A few seconds later violins filled the air. I gave her a smile as we slowly made our way to the aisle. I had no idea she was going to play music for me to walk down the aisle to.

I felt my knees go weak when I saw Garrett for the first time. He was dressed in a blue suit with a burgundy and purple tie. His short dark hair glinted under the white lights, and I could tell he'd recently shaved. He looked so handsome I almost forgot to breathe.

"Almost there," Doc whispered. "Keep moving."

My face split into a wide grin, and I knew I probably looked insane. But I didn't care. At that particular moment I'd never been so happy. I was surrounded by people who loved me and wanted only the best for me.

I glanced at Aunt Shirley, but she only had eyes for Old Man Jenkins. Paige was softly crying and looked lovingly at Matt, who was standing behind Garrett. Mom wiped her eyes and gave me a watery smile. I also didn't miss the way she looked adoringly at Doc.

At that precise moment, I didn't know how my life could get any better.

"Dearly beloved," Hank began.

Oh, yeah. I know how. Hank was officiating my wedding.

I forced myself to stop daydreaming and listen to Hank.

"Who gives this woman away?" Hank asked.

"We do," Doc and Old Man Jenkins replied.

They each gave me a kiss on the cheek then offered my hand to Garrett. I clasped my hand around Garrett's and held on for dear life. He squeezed my hand and smiled reassuringly at me.

Twenty of our closest family and friends watched as Garrett and I declared our love for each other and Hank pronounced us man and wife. I cried even though I said I wouldn't.

By the time six o'clock rolled around and Mindy had taken a hundred pictures, I was ready to let loose and party. The catered food was fabulous, the music was lively, and the drinks were flowing. I caught a glimpse of Old Man Jenkins and Aunt Shirley boogieing down on the dance floor and laughed.

"What's so funny, wife?"

I grinned and wrapped my arms around Garrett's neck. "Mmm…I could get used to you calling me that."

He laughed. "I should hope so. We're married now, you know?"

"Is that what that ceremony meant?"

He swatted me playfully on the butt, but I didn't feel a thing with the size of the wedding dress.

"We've already cut the cake," Garrett said. "And we've tossed the bouquet and garter. Is there anything else we have to do?"

I played with the back of his neck. "Well, there is one more tradition on the wedding night we haven't done yet."

Garrett's eyes turned dark. "Is it okay if we leave now?"

Garrett's mom and dad were supposed to stay the night at the Granville Hotel, but Mom wouldn't have it. Now that Danner had been caught and Paige and Matt could go back to their house, it left two bedrooms unused. Mom had insisted that Garrett's parents stay with her. Which meant Garrett and I could be alone our first night as husband and wife.

Aunt Shirley and Old Man Jenkins sauntered over to where Garrett and I were entwined.

"Pretty good turn out," Aunt Shirley said. "I'd say there're about a hundred and twenty people here."

"I know. It's crazy," I said.

We all stood quietly and watched the crowd. There were people on the dance floor dancing, while others were sitting at the tables still piecing at the food. Everyone looked to be enjoying themselves.

"I don't see Willa or her mom," Aunt Shirley chuckled.

"Hey, that reminds me," Garrett said, turning to face me. "Claire radioed me as I was driving over for the wedding ceremony and said Willa Trindle had called the station to report that I needed to arrest you for public intoxication and outright craziness."

I giggled. "I might have gone over the edge a little when I went to question her right before we went to the cemetery."

"A *little*," Aunt Shirley guffawed. "Girl, you jumped right over the edge of that cliff and screamed all the way down."

"Do I want to know?" Garrett asked.

I shook my head. "Nope."

Garrett leaned over and gave me a hard smack on the lips. "Mrs. Kimble, try to contain yourself in public, will you? I'd hate to have to arrest you."

I grinned up at him. "I'll try."

"Hey, containing yourself reminds me," Aunt Shirley said. "Now, try to contain yourself, but I have one last gift for you two."

Garrett and I groaned at the same time.

"Hey now!" Aunt Shirley exclaimed as Old Man Jenkins laughed.

"Did I hear someone say they were getting one last gift?" Hank asked as he and Mindy sauntered over to our little group. He lifted his hand in the air and motioned Matt, Paige, Mom and Doc over.

"What's going on?" I asked suspiciously.

"I might have let the others in on the surprise," Aunt Shirley said eagerly. "I just couldn't keep it to myself anymore."

Matt slapped Garrett on the back and Mom mouthed she was sorry.

"What's going on?" I demanded again.

"Well, the old man and I—"

160

"Don't you drag me into this," Old Man Jenkins joked. "I said no, but you insisted."

"What?" Garrett demanded.

Aunt Shirley reached down inside her bra and pulled out a couple envelopes.

I wrinkled my nose. "Have you had those there the whole night?"

Aunt Shirley grinned. "Sure have. Wanted to keep them safe and secure."

"What are they?" Garrett asked suspiciously.

Hank chuckled again and Mindy hit him in the arm. "Behave yourself, Hank."

Aunt Shirley plunked down the envelopes in Garrett's hand. He opened up one of the envelopes and stared, his brow furrowed.

"What is it?" I asked.

Garrett shrugged. "It looks like a ticket for Aunt Shirley and Jenkins to go on some kind of a train ride."

"What's the other one say?" Hank asked, still grinning like a fool.

Garrett gave me a guarded look. "Do I want to open this?"

"Probably not," I whispered.

"Open it!" Aunt Shirley cried.

"Here." Doc handed Garrett a beer. "You might need this."

Garrett handed me the envelope. "You open it."

Aunt Shirley playfully slapped Garrett's arm. "Oh, now. You're gonna love it!"

I slowly opened the envelope and read.

"No." Garrett shook his head. His face pale in the moonlight.

"What is it?" Hank asked again.

I never wanted to punch Hank so hard in all my life.

"It's a ticket for you to join us on the train ride!" Aunt Shirley cried. "We're gonna do a double honeymoon!"

My mouth dropped open. "Aunt Shirley, Garrett and I decided to put off going on a honeymoon for a few months."

"Nonsense," Aunt Shirley said. "I already checked and Garrett has plenty of leave, and Hank is *thrilled* at the thought of us doing a double honeymoon. Aren't ya, Hank?"

Hank grinned and nodded. "I'm ecstatic. I want to know all the details."

I narrowed my eyes at him. "You're such a bully."

Hank winked at me and took a swig of his beer.

"Well," I said. "I guess we're going on a train ride for a honeymoon next weekend."

A cry of joy went up…from everyone but Garrett and me. I was still in shock. Garrett had already moved ahead in his stages of grief to denial and bargaining.

"I think I have a seminar I have to attend," Garrett said lamely. "Maybe we can do this in a couple months."

Aunt Shirley gave him the evil eye. "Garrett Kimble, I know for a fact you have nothing on your calendar for the next few weeks. I'm a pretty good detective, and I've ferreted this information out for myself."

"It's only for four days," I said. "Surely we can do four days."

"Four days…on a train…for our honeymoon…with Aunt Shirley and Jenkins," Garrett said between clenched teeth. "Sure. We can do these four days standing on our head."

Aunt Shirley clapped her hands in glee. "Wonderful! This is the perfect ending to a perfect day. Could it get any better?"

"Maybe," Paige said weakly.

"What's wrong?" Matt asked, suddenly on alert.

Paige looked down at the ground. "I think my water just broke!"

ABOUT THE AUTHOR

Jenna writes in the genre of cozy/women's literature. Her humorous characters and stories revolve around over-the-top family members, creative murders, and there's always a positive element of the military in her stories. Jenna currently lives in Missouri with her fiancé, step-daughter, Nova Scotia duck tolling retriever dog, Brownie, and her tuxedo-cat, Whiskey. She is a former court reporter turned educator turned full-time writer. She has a Master's degree in Special Education, and an Education Specialist degree in Curriculum and Instruction. She also spent twelve years in full-time ministry.

When she's not writing, Jenna likes to attend beer and wine tastings, go antiquing, visit craft festivals, and spend time with her family and friends. You can friend request her on Facebook under Jenna St. James, and she has a blog http://jennastjames.blogspot.com/. You can also e-mail her at authorjennastjames@gmail.com.

Jenna writes both the Ryli Sinclair Mystery and the Sullivan Sisters Mystery. You can purchase these books at http://amazon.com/author/jennastjames. Thank you for taking the time to read Jenna St. James' books. If you enjoy her books, please leave a review on Amazon, Goodreads, or any other social media outlet.

Made in the USA
Columbia, SC
25 August 2018